SIMON SON OF STAR

Adapted from the multi award-winning
screenplay by Ronen Tergerman & Jack Snyder

By

Ronen Tregerman

In loving memory of Maria Herlinda Hernandez (Linda), our beloved grandmother, mother, mother-in-law and sister. You were always my biggest fan, always encouraging me to keep on writing even at times I was ready to lay down my pen.

Contents

Have you ever taken the time to look closely at a coin? Our currency, any coin, look closely and you will find that throughout time we mint our coins with our faith, goals, dreams, leaders, sovereignty, and legacy.

We mount and press our dreams and visions on a hard currency and precious metal, deeming it valuable and hoping for it to last forever. This story is about a coin from the Holy Land minted nearly two-thousand years ago. A heroic story of courage against all odds that has become a legend through the millennia.

Prologue

A white-gloved hand opened the top of a display case, then carefully lifted an ancient silver coin. But as he held it up, it slipped from his fingers and clattered to the concrete floor. The eight members of the tour group simultaneously gasped.

Jacob Ponson bent down to retrieve it. But the curator, a stuffy proper man in his fifties, shouted, "Don't touch!" He quickly moved around the pedestal and bent over, his face reddened and his neck bulged against his bowtie as he picked up the coin with his gloved hand. He stood up and offered the tour members an embarrassed grin. "Fortunately, the director didn't see that. First time I ever dropped it. The gloves are a bit slippery." He turned to Jacob. "Sorry to shout, but this is an extremely rare coin with an unusual history."

"Understood. I'm well aware, sir."

Jacob, who was forty-four and smartly dressed in a violet Prada cashmere polo shirt and black slacks, had asked to see this very coin when he arrived. He was trim and confident with an air of wealth. The curator had simply nodded toward the assembled rotary club tour and told him that he could join them and they would all get to see the coin.

"Come closer, everyone. I want you to take a good look at this coin. He held it up, revealing an image of the Ark of the Covenant and Hebrew words that Jacob knew said: *Simon President of Israel.* Jacob pulled out his magnifying glass to get a closer look, but before he could focus on it, the curator turned the coin over and pushed it so close that Jacob had to lower the magnifying glass. He peered at the image of a temple and a rising star, and the motto in Hebrew: *For the Freedom of Jerusalem.*

The curator pulled out his own magnifying glass and held it in front of the coin. "Please let's all take a closer look." Jacob stepped aside so the others could see better. When the viewers had seen enough, the curator placed the coin back in the display case. "Now, we can proceed to the adjoining media room where you can watch a fascinating twenty-minute video about ancient Israeli history, including the story behind this coin that I just showed you."

Jacob had seen that YouTube video several times and decided to skip it. He had another idea to pursue. He moved back toward the front of the museum. Ancient artwork from the Middle East adorned the walls. Statues stood frozen in time behind velvet ropes and display cases held ancient trinkets. Jacob made his way to the entrance where a young woman greeted visitors, collected a ten-dollar fee, and handed out brochures. While she tended to a pair of new visitors, he opened his copy of the brochure and read the introduction to the exhibition.

The centerpiece of this exhibit is a coin from nearly two-thousand years ago. A coin from the Holy Land in the center of a story of faith, courage, and a fight against overwhelming odds.

"Excuse me," he said and smiled at the woman after the visitors moved inside. "I'd like to speak to the museum director."

She quickly looked him over. "Of course. Could I tell him the reason for your visit?"

"It's about the coin. I'm a collector." He told her his name as if it would mean something to the director.

"Oh, I'll text Dr. Holmes." She tapped on her cellphone, then raised her gaze. "He usually replies within a minute or so. She'd no sooner spoken when her phone chimed. "Oh, that was fast." She studied her phone for a few moments, then smiled. "You can make an appointment for after lunch, or the director can give you five minutes right now, if you prefer that."

"That should be plenty."

"Good. Follow me."

"Come in," a gravelly voice called out after Jacob's guide tapped on the director's door. He sat at an oversized mahogany desk and stared at a computer screen as Jacob stepped up to him. Holmes mumbled something about an email as he typed, and Jacob waited patiently.

"Done." Holmes stood up, extended a hand, leaned across his desk, and then told Jacob to take a seat. He was at least a decade older than Jacob and he wore a beard threaded with gray. His round auburn glass frames had slipped down his nose revealing bushy eyebrows. His suit coat covered the hint of a bulging belly.

He closed the cover of his laptop and crossed his arms. "How can I help you, Mr. Ponson?"

"The coin captivated me the first time I saw it in a museum in Jerusalem, the image of the Holy Temple, the Ark of the Covenant, and a single star struck on the face of it."

Holmes nodded and leaned back in his chair as Jacob continued.

"I've been searching for one like it ever since, all over the world. Galleries. Antique dealers. But the coin always seems to be one step ahead of me, sold to a museum or a collector just before I arrived. Like the coin in your museum now."

Holmes smiled and brought his palms together. "Well, you're in luck. There is an identical coin being presented at a Heritage auction in Long Beach, California, in a couple of weeks."

Jacob's eyes widened. He'd hoped that Holmes might give him the name of a collector or two who owned identical coins and who might be willing to sell for the right price. But an auction was much preferred. His search might finally be over.

⌘

Jacob found himself in the midst of a huge coin auction at the Long Beach Convention Center that attracted buyers from around the world.

The ancient Judean coins, though, were being auctioned in a relatively small room, separate from the main auction. It was obviously a specialty room with its marble flooring, mahogany walls, and chandeliers. Jacob was one of about thirty buyers. Some were private collectors like himself, others were coin dealers. There were also museum buyers, including one from the Israel Museum in Jerusalem. Some represented buyers from around the world, who weren't present but were on their phones or the internet.

A few dozen ancient coins were up for auction and all were assigned a lot number and auctioned in order. Jacob knew the number of his coin and that it would come up in about the middle of the auction. He'd been allowed to examine the coin closely yesterday, and as he'd held it in his hand, a ripple of excitement passed through him. He'd instantly known he had to win this very unique coin; made of silver, with the front inscribed with the image of the Holy Temple and in the center the Ark of Covenant. The only coin ever made with the image of the ark on it and the holy temple. And its condition was so remarkable that he knew nothing was going to stop him from taking this coin home.

Jacob waited patiently and after an hour and a half, the auctioneer spoke the magical words into the microphone that he'd been waiting to hear. "A silver Bar Kochva Revolt coin." The auctioneer, a man in his forties dressed in business casual – a sport jacket over an open-collared shirt - motioned to his assistant, a woman in her twenties, who held up the coin. The image instantly popped up on a large screen above the stage. "Issued by the Judean rebel state during the Bar Kochva Revolt against the Roman Empire circa 134/135 AD. Near mint condition."

The assistant rotated it. All eyes focused on the screen as the magnificent coin glistened in the assistant's hand. "Only a few remain in the world in such pristine condition," the auctioneer continued. "Opening bid, seventy-five-hundred dollars. Do I hear..."

A woman in the crowd raised a large white card with the number 45 in large black print.

"We have seventy-five-hundred dollars," the auctioneer said, nodding to the woman.

"Do I hear eight thousand? Jacob raises his card. It was numbered 32.

"We have eight-thousand. Do I hear eighty-five-hundred?"

A man held up number 18. The woman who opened the bidding frowned and shook her head.

"Do I hear nine-thousand?"

Jacob, stoic and undaunted, raised his card.

"How about ninety-five-hundred?"

Another man showed his card, bidding for the first time.

"Ten thousand?"

Jacob raised his card again. He was unconcerned. But he noticed a man standing off to the side, curiously watching from the shadows. He had a silver-threaded goatee and was trimly built. Dressed in black, he wore a black cap pulled forward as if the lights were too bright for his eyes.

"Do I hear ten-five?" the auctioneer called out.

No card-bearing hands were raised. The auctioneer glanced around. Going once... going twice... Sold to number thirty-two for ten thousand dollars."

Half an hour later, Jacob stood in the corridor outside the small auction room. He gingerly unwrapped a felt cloth and gazed upon the coin. His treasure. Smiling, he made his way down the corridor, his shoes echoing on the marble floor.

The man that he'd noticed earlier was leaning against the wall, watching him approach.

"Congrats on the coin," the man said. Jacob glanced over with trepidation. What did this person want? The man offered him a genuine, warm smile, putting him at ease. "Are you a collector of antiquities in general? Or is that coin special?"

"Both." Jacob could see the man's eyes now and realized he was not only older but also posed no threat.

"Interesting. What is it about that coin?"

"I'm a student of Judean history with a particular fascination of the events surrounding this coin."

"Really?" He slightly tilted his head to the side. "If you have a moment, can you indulge me with that history?"

Something about the way he asked suggested he already knew. Jacob chuckled. "Well, it's a long story."

"I'd love to hear it..." He'd almost said the word 'again,' Jacob thought. It occurred to him that the mysterious man, who was so curious about the coin and its history, might be its former owner. But he didn't ask. Maybe Jacob didn't want to know. "Sure. As a matter of fact, I enjoy telling it." He gazed off, as if staring back into time to a distant land.

"It began in Rome... in 132 A.D... during a Senate meeting with Emperor Hadrian..."

Chapter 1

Emperor Hadrian waited patiently in the Curia Julia, the Senate's chambers, for his senators and generals to take their seats. The Curia was built 150 years ago by Julius Caesar replacing an older Curia, but Caesar didn't live to see it completed. Ironically, he was assassinated in the Curia of Pompey where the Senate was meeting during the re-construction.

Hadrian gazed off toward the far end of the hall where a statue of Victoria, the personification of victory, stood on a globe, extending a wreath. When the senators entering the chamber blocked his view, he turned his gaze to the floor, the only other unique feature of the building. Made in an art technique, *opus sectile,* the floor featured pearls, marble, and glass cut and inlaid to make pictures or patterns of red, green, and purple squares and rectangles.

His thoughts drifted back to the loss of his lover, Antinous, who had drowned in the Nile River a year ago. He'd never encountered anyone of such beauty and had never felt so deeply in love with anyone. He'd wept at his loss, even wept in public. Antinous had accompanied Hadrian on his tours of the Roman Empire and if Hadrian hadn't taken him to the Nile, he might still be alive. His death was a mystery and Hadrian feared that he might've committed suicide because of a harsh comment he'd made to his lover the night before. Now statues of Antinous were being built throughout Hadrian's empire. Antinous would be deified, worshipped as a god, and Hadrian even had plans for a new city to be named Antinoplis, which would be founded on the banks of the Nile near the site of his death.

But he wasn't here today to talk about Antinous. Another important issue was on his mind. He watched his decorated generals and the toga-clad senators chatter as they sat on a semi-circle of benches facing Hadrian who was draped in a purple toga indicative of his elite status and seated on a raised platform on his portable curule seat that was made of ivory. Far from a throne, it was a stool without a back and with curved legs that could be folded.

Hadrian gazed over the chattering and commiserating senators, wondering which ones were secretly planning to undermine his rule. He turned his attention to General Sextus Severus, letting him know that he was ready to begin. Severus was a trusted military leader, who had served as governor of Moesia, and for the past year as governor of Britain. But Hadrian had called him back to Rome for this meeting and had asked him to assume the temporary role of presiding magistrate of the senate. He hoped that would appease the general when he found out he was losing his new governorship.

Severus stood up and stepped forward. "The senate meeting is called to order." The room fell silent. The senators all stared at Hadrian attentive and expressionless. He knew that many of them despised him and all feared him. One of his first acts upon becoming emperor in 117 A.D., after the death of his adoptive father, Trajan, was to order the execution of four top-ranked senators who he thought were a threat to his leadership.

Severus ceremoniously recited a formal greeting that all presiding magistrates said when addressing Hadrian at the beginning of senate meetings. "If you and your children are well, all is well. For I and the army are in good health."

Hadrian tensed at the word 'children' but quickly hid his annoyance. He smiled and nodded. He actually liked the introduction. When he heard Severus say, *For I and my army are in good health*, it made him feel good because the strength of the army showed that he was the commander of the greatest army in the world.

He glanced around the room again at the assembled senators to see if any were snickering, then back to Severus. "What do my generals have for me?"

Severus motioned to Generals Gaius Publicius and Haterius Nepos, both hardened military leaders in their fifties. They joined Severus on the floor, and the three honored generals bowed to Hadrian. Publicius took a tentative step forward. "The Roman army - the greatest army of all time - has broken all resistance throughout Europe, Your Majesty."

Hadrian narrowed his gaze. "And our province of Judea?"

Nepos, a short stocky man and the most affable of the thr ee generals, puffed out his chest and lifted up on his toes to increase his stature. "Rome has full control of the Levant and Jerusalem."

Hadrian pursed his lips and stared hard at Nepos. "My spies have said there are talks of rebellion. What do you know about it?"

"There is some such talk in the villages, but all indications are that it is very disorganized with no leader. Nothing to be concerned about at this point."

"Let's keep it that way." Hadrian turned quiet, lost in thought for a few moments. Then he focused on Nepos again. "Do the people of Jerusalem still worship their unseen god?"

Nepos nodded. "Yes, Your Majesty. Unfortunately, the Judeans refuse to believe in the Roman gods." He paused a moment, smirked. "And they continue their ancient practice of circumcision as a covenant with their god."

"How barbaric." The emperor stood up from his curule seat and gazed down at his three military leaders. "General Nepos, send a legion to Judea, to all their cities with orders banning circumcision. Violation of such is punishable by death."

He paced the platform, his mind working, all eyes on him. He scanned the senators, again wondering about who the secret enemies among them were. He returned his attention to the generals.

"Enforce pagan law over their land, as it is mine now. And change Jerusalem's name to Aelia Capitolina, a capital to the Roman god, Jupiter. I want to see monuments dedicated to him all over the city!"

"Yes, Your Majesty. It will be done immediately," Nepos responded.

Hadrian looked past Nepos to the seated senators and glared at them. He knew that some of them gossiped that he, Hadrian, unlike previous emperors, had made no effort to expand the empire. He saw no point in it. His concern was maintaining and protecting the empire, building fortifications, temples, and monuments. To do so, he traveled frequently, more so than any previous emperors.

He had visited the far corner of the empire from Egypt to Britain, and all of the provinces. Greece, by far, was his favorite. He had been an admirer of Greek culture since his youth and was even called *Graeculus* – Little Greek - because of his love for Athens and Hellenic culture. The Greeks and the Romans shared the same gods, though with different names. Hadrian was the only emperor who wore a beard, and he did so in honor of the Greek philosophers.

He'd taken Antinous to Greece and also to Judea on the same trip where he would later die. Hadrian wanted Judea to be more like Greece, but the people of Judea continued to reject him and his rule as well as any efforts to Hellenize them. But now they would find out how much that angered him.

Following the meeting with his generals and senators, Hadrian returned to the palace on Palatine Hill. He much preferred his villa at Tibur outside the city and the meeting was the only reason he was staying at the palace today. Servants followed in his wake as he strode through the grand hallway. He found the empress relaxing on a couch as servants tended to her. She looked up as he approached. "How did it go today, my love?"

Vibia Sabina was the grand-niece of Trajan, the former emperor. She was well aware of Hadrian's dealings and often traveled with him. He had married Sabina twelve years ago, the same year that he'd built his villa as his getaway from the pressures of ruling in Rome. Married at seventeen, she had assumed the role of empress with grace and surprising ease. In their years together, she had accumulated more public honors in Rome and the provinces than any imperial Roman woman before her. At Hadrian's order, her image was featured on a series of coins minted in Rome. Four years ago, she had been awarded the title of Augusta, an honorific title for imperial women that implied great prestige.

Hadrian dismissed all the servants and they quickly scuttled away. "The Senate doesn't show me respect."

Sabina looked amused. "You always say that."

"It's true."

"Well, you did put several of them to death."

Hadrian frowned defensively. "They opposed my succession to the throne. They were plotting against me from the beginning. I had to show my power and determination to rule."

Sabina shrugged. "I'm not defending them. I'm just stating a fact."

His empress was loyal, but he knew from his loyal servants that privately she made comments about his behavior with young men, and that offended him. She had told him that she was sorry about Antinous' death, but she also seemed relieved that he was gone. His relationship with Sabina was formal and one of appearance. An emperor needed an empress, but there was no joy in their intimate relations. It was a process to make children and she'd failed him.

"The presiding magistrate always begin the session by stating if my children are well, then all is well. So I designated General Severus as the magistrate today, and can you believe it, he said the same offensive words. It grates on me." He eyed her with blame and her smile faltered.

"It's just a formality. They mean nothing by it. And we may yet conceive," she replied in a calm voice and a forced smile.

Hadrian's gaze narrowed as he peered at her, his lips pursed. Then his featured relaxed. "Yes, that would be good. Would it not?" With that, he turned and walked away. Her smile had faded with his words and he knew she was glaring at him from behind his back. He didn't care.

Chapter 2

THE CENTURION AND HIS TROOPS thundered toward the provincial village, a cloud of dust rising in their wake. Stone and wooden structures were clustered at the center, and others were spread out across the land. The denizens went about their business, working, perusing the market, men led mules that pulled carts. Abruptly, they all stopped what they were doing and turned toward the village entrance.

Clavius and his eighty legionnaires stampeded into the village, sending everyone shouting and screaming, scrambling for cover as they charged into the center of the Judean outpost. He carried a three-foot long vine-staff, a sign of his position as a centurion and also a handy weapon to beat resistant citizens. He wore a bronze and iron breastplate, chainmail, and a special helmet with a large horsehair plume on it.

Clavius trotted in a circle looking out for any villagers who might be foolish enough to attack the troops. But everyone remained out of sight. "Come forward!" he shouted. "I have an announcement to make."

No one appeared. He would wait. Eventually, some curious villagers emerged from their hiding places and looked cautiously toward the Romans when they saw that the soldiers weren't pillaging the village but waiting to talk to them.

Like most centurions, Clavius was of plebian origin and had been promoted from the ranks of the common soldiers. He was in his early thirties, broad and muscular, a head taller than most of his soldiers. His advancement to the centurion he knew was related to the fact that stood out among his men. The centurions were the backbone of the legion and were responsible for enforcing discipline in the provinces. Judea was no exception and the reprisals would be harsh if the populace didn't obey the proclamations.

He was proud of his position, was paid more than regular soldiers, and was ready to enforce whatever orders came down from the emperor and his generals. He enjoyed the feeling of power he wielded since assuming his role five years ago, but he was also aware of two important factors. If he abused his troops, they could turn on him and he could be demoted to an ordinary soldier again. Besides that, he knew that his power and sense of independence all depended on his following orders exactly as he was told by his superiors.

After a few minutes, several men stepped forward. Their leader, a village elder with long white hair and a matching beard, crossed his arms and frowned at Clavius, a defiant look on his deeply tanned wrinkled features. He felt like laughing at him but decided that respect – at least for the moment – would serve him better. The old man and the others would spread the word to the villagers and beyond.

"The emperor has issued an edict!" he called out. "No more worshiping of your deity! From this moment, you are under pagan rule."

The old man wasn't deterred by Clavius's recitation of Hadrian's proclamation. "Our God is superior to your many gods. Our religion, our faith, is our history, and it won't be eliminated."

"Where is your temple?" Clavius demanded.

The men shook their heads "We are a small village. We have no temple here in Arpha," one of them said.

Clavius laughed. "So you have no place to worship your invisible god."

"We worship in the next town, Gophna, an hour's ride." He motioned in a southerly direction.

Clavius scowled and pointed his vine-staff at him. "If you're lying, I will be back." With that, he led his troops out of the village.

Clavius was angered by the insolence of the villagers of Arpha, so when they charged into Gophna, he made no effort to stop and read the emperor's edict. He kept riding until he found the village synagogue. He and his legionnaires dismounted and stormed through the front doors. The rabbi and his worshippers, startled by the sudden intrusion, turned and gaped.

"What is going on here?" the rabbi shouted. "This is a house of worship. You have no place here."

"From now on, you worship the Roman gods," Clavius shouted as his soldiers moved forward, awaiting orders."

"There is only one god, the God," the rabbi responded.

"Then you can worship Jupiter, the sky-god, who oversees everything – all aspects of life." Clavius moved forward and ordered his soldiers to gather the holy books. They quickly scooped up Torah scrolls from a table. The rabbi ordered them to stop but was pushed away. The worshippers shouted and cried out, then hurried after the soldiers as they abandoned the temple with the sacred texts.

The scrolls were hurled into a pile in the road outside the door. A crowd quickly gathered and Clavius shouted, "You are now pagans and circumcision is illegal, as ordered by the emperor."

Shouts and chants of "Never! Never!" arose.

In response, Clavius grabbed a torch a soldier had lit and jammed it into the holy books. The rabbi and several men grabbed for the scrolls in an attempt to spare them from the flames. Clavius slammed his vine-staff against the hands of one of the men who had reached into the fire. The scroll he'd snatched fell back into the fire and one of the soldiers ran him through with his sword.

The crowd screamed in horror and rushed forward and the soldiers responded by slashing and stabbing. Blood spilled and stained the dirt road and the scrolls blackened, burned, and turned to ash. The survivors dragged the dead and injured away as soldiers with swords drawn formed a line in front of the fire.

"Let this be a warning!" Clavius shouted after the retreating villagers. "Changes are coming to all of Judea. So says Emperor Hadrian!"

After days of galloping into villages and towns and confronting denizens with Rome's harsh new rules aimed at eliminating the Judean religion, Clavius and his troops made their way toward Jerusalem. He was impressed by the scenic landscape – the mountains and verdant valleys that surrounded the high plateau where the city was perched between the Dead Sea and the Mediterranean.

Clavius and his troops approached the city and were greeted by Roman soldiers. He knew that much of the city had been destroyed when the Romans captured it more than sixty years ago. But the residents had been allowed to rebuild destroyed buildings and homes, except for their holy temple. That site remained empty but soon that would change when a statue of Jupiter would mark the land as Roman property.

He held up an arm signaling his troops to stop near the market. Clavius remained on horseback as he shouted that he would read a new proclamation by Emperor Hadrian. The citizens, who had been perusing rows of tents packed with a variety of goods – clothing, food, utensils, and jewelry – stopped what they were doing and turned to the new arrivals.

Clavius unfurled a scroll and looked over the gathering crowd. "By order of His Majesty Emperor Hadrian, effective immediately, there will be no more circumcision. There will be…" A voice in the crowd interrupted him. "We've already heard this from you Romans. We don't agree, do we?"

A chorus of shouts drowned out any attempt at continuing to read the proclamation. Some were angry, others weeping in despair. When it was apparent they wouldn't quiet down to allow him to speak and that they already knew about the proclamation, Clavius motioned to his soldiers to follow him. He led them farther into the city, single-file through narrow streets and passages until they came to a temple.

Clavius remained mounted and passively watched as his soldiers burned down the place of worship. When a rabbi and worshippers ran out, he shouted: "Your Judea religion will be replaced by the beliefs of Rome." Even though a resistance force could easily close off any escape for his troops in the enclosed city streets, Clavius had no concern about retaliation. The people seemed too stunned to act and were intimidated by the mounted soldiers, who waved swords and awaited any challenges. But how long would that last? He wondered.

As the days went by and Clavius remained in Jerusalem, he longed to go home to his wife and two children. He hadn't seen them in more than six months and was due time off from his service to the emperor. He had submitted without complaint to this mission because he understood that he and his *centuria* were in Judea to spread the word of the emperor's orders, not to remain and enforce them. But now General Severus said that the people of Judea had been stirred up and were showing signs of preparation to take action. That was not the news that Clavius wanted to hear.

Severus had addressed all the centurions in Jerusalem and told them they would be staying in the province of Judea to put down any attempts to retaliate. When the general had asked the centurions if they had any questions or concerns, Clavius had boldly addressed him, saying that his soldiers were overdue to be relieved on the field and that he had told them they would only be here to spread Hadrian's orders.

"The mission has changed," Severus responded. "The emperor has ordered a legion to Judea. You are just the spearhead. And we will still need you and your soldiers."

Clavius stood stoically at attention without expression on his face, but inside he was seething. *How much longer would he and his soldiers be forced to remain in the field, another six months, a year?*

To his surprise, Severus walked over to him. "Because of your service, Centurion, I am promoting you. You will be in charge of an entire cohort. Do you understand?"

Clavius was stunned by the sudden advancement. A cohort consisted of six *centuria* and there were ten cohorts in a legion for a total of 6, 000 soldiers. Now, instead of being one of sixty centurions in a legion, he was one of ten leaders of the cohorts. Severus, he realized, had cleverly shifted his concerns about going home to taking a new leadership role. He was grateful and knew he would also get a boost in pay. He just hoped he would live long enough to enjoy his substantial wages.

Clavius didn't need his entire cohort to attend to one particular task that Severus had ordered him to carry out. So, he'd told the five centurions now under his command to remain in the encampment outside the city and send out patrols to watch for any unusual movement of people and to inspect carts coming into the city for weapons.

Now he watched from his stead as several soldiers struggled to erect a 20-foot-tall statue of the Roman god Jupiter on Temple Mount at the remains of the holy temple of Israel. He kept an eye on the crowd gathering around the ruins, located at the highest site in the city. Foot soldiers surrounded the platform forming a barrier between workers raising the statue and the crowd. Several troublemakers were shouting curses and telling everyone approaching that the Romans were defiling sacred ground.

Clavius couldn't put up with it any longer. He trotted over to the crowd. "Statues honoring the great Roman gods are being erected throughout the capital and all of Judea. Here in the most honored site in the Judea Quarter of Jerusalem will stand the image of the god, Jupiter. You should pray to him and ask for good luck in your life. He has the power to bring it to you."

"Your gods bow to the one God," someone yelled out. "That's the only God we praise."

Clavius spotted the speaker who stood in the midst of the crowd and saw that he was elderly and his robes identified him as a rabbi. He would like to swat him with his vine-staff but it would be too much trouble reaching him in the crowd. Instead, he turned his attention back to the soldiers struggling with the enormous statue. They tugged on half a dozen taut ropes that were anchored to the platform as they wrestled it up to its pedestal. It hovered at an angle as they meticulously worked to get it upright.

Clavius shouted for the men to pull harder, that they almost had it. That was when something in the distance caught his attention. He squinted and saw that about a hundred paces away, a tall, muscular-built man stood alone on the slope leading to the site. None of the people who had gathered to watch and complain about the erection of the statue seemed to notice him. But even at this distance, Clavius sensed something about the figure that made him wary. His fists-on-hips posture telegraphed a charismatic confidence that set him apart from any other person who were protesting against the Romans and their rules. And he appeared to be staring straight at Clavius. It was a bit unnerving.

He turned to the soldier nearest him. "Munifex, do we know that man who's watching us?" He pointed him out.

"No sir. I've never seen him. He's not one of ours."

Clavius called over a few soldiers. "I want three of you to ride over and see…."

"Ah, sir, he's running toward us," Munifex said.

Everyone looked. Sure enough, the man was rushing in their direction like a charging bull. The determination in the man's demeanor didn't sit well with Clavius. Best to finish him right now before he caused any trouble.

"Archers! Drop that man!" Clavius shouted.

A half-dozen mounted archers drew their bows back and launched arrows at the moving target. The running man was fit and appeared nearly as large and muscular as Clavius. He was dressed lightly, not for combat. He dodged the rain of arrows with ease and continued advancing toward Clavius and the soldiers. The men pulling on the ropes had stopped to watch and the statue of Jupiter rocked unsteadily at the edge of the platform.

When the man was close enough for the archers to fire straight at him, he snatched a plank of wood in his path and used it as a shield. The arrows thumped harmlessly into the wood. He kept coming and the archers kept firing with the same results as the plank collected arrows. Then he was too close for the archers to fire on him. His piercing eyes focused on Clavius, who was impressed with the man's boldness and his brawn. His jaw dropped as he realized the man was unarmed. "Munifex! Stop him!"

"Yes, sir." The soldier looked warily at the charging man, then withdrew his sword, and bolted toward him.

"Everyone! Your swords!" Clavius shouted to the foot soldiers and men holding the ropes. Then he turned back to the approaching figure. *What did he want? What was wrong with him? Did he want to die for his one god?*

A dozen soldiers unsheathed their swords just as the brash intruder and Munifex met atop the mount and engaged. He must be crazy or just ready to die for his cause, Clavius thought.

"My name is Simon, the last name you will ever hear," the man called out. In response,

Munifex swung his sword at his unarmed opponent. But Simon was skilled and dexterous. He dodged and ducked. Swing after swing, Munifex missed, and it seemed that his opponent somehow cleverly appeared, disappeared, and reappeared several feet away. Clavius and the others watched in awe and a bit of fear as the man who called himself Simon effortlessly evaded the razor-sharp blade.

Suddenly and swiftly, he moved in and grappled with Munifex. He quickly disarmed him and snatched up the sword. Without a moment's hesitation, he jammed the blade through Munifex's chest, killing him instantly.

Clavius gasped and angrily jabbed a finger toward Simon. "Kill him! Kill him now!"

With that, six soldiers rushed Simon and surrounded him, but none seemed willing to take him on alone. Outnumbered but undaunted, Simon charged toward two of the soldiers. Metal flashed and glistened in the sun as swords clanged. Simon moved with the gracefulness of a seasoned, expert dancer as he twirled around in a blur, fatally slicing one soldier after the next with the deadly steel in his hand. When only one was left, the soldier dropped his sword and held up his hands. He took a couple steps back, ready to turn and run for his life, but Simon leaped forward and with a single swipe of his new sword cleanly removed the man's head.

With the last soldier dead, his sightless eyes staring at the sky, Simon kicked the head like a ball. Then he picked up the bloody headless body and held it in front of him using it as a shield as the archers fired again, every volley striking the dead soldier. Simon continued forward toward Clavius and the archers.

"Get off your horses!" Clavius shouted at the archers. With their enemy too close to use bows, they hastily dismounted and drew short swords. Clavius could see the terror in their eyes. Simon dropped the body and rushed forward. Unfortunately for the archers, they lacked skill with the blade and Simon finished them off quickly.

He advanced on Clavius, and the brawny centurion expertly slipped off his horse with a sword in hand. He glanced back at the soldiers who had been working on the statue. None of them were armed and none of them looked ready to come to his aid. Just in time, Clavius swung his sword and met Simon's stolen blade.

Though Simon was imposing, Clavius was just as robust, even taller and heavier. They circled each other, clashed and withdrew their swords. As they parried, Simon smiled, seemingly enjoying the challenge.

"Who are you?" Clavius asked.

Simon didn't answer. Instead, he moved in close, too close for Clavius' sword to be effective. Simon swiftly and deftly jammed his sword inches from Clavius' hand, and dislodged his weapon, sending it tumbling away in the dirt. Clavius looked over at it, but he knew that Simon would gut him before he took a step to retrieve the sword. The moment of his death had arrived and his thoughts flashed to his wife and two young sons and he wondered what would become of them. He glimpsed them for an instant before Simon swept him off his feet with the nimble swing of a leg. And he fell onto his back.

The point of Simon's blade hovered in front of Clavius' face, and he dared not move. The blade touched his throat as Simon addressed him. "Tell your emperor this city has only one God!" To Clavius' surprise, Simon darted away. He sat up just in time to see the mysterious intruder slicing the ropes one after another that held the statue of Jupiter at an angle to the pedestal. As he cut the last one, the statue toppled and shattered on the ground, the head breaking off.

Clavius took advantage of the moment and started crawling toward his sword but the nimble killer jumped from the pedestal and dashed over, and stepped on the blade before Clavius could pick it up. "My name is Simon ben Kosevah. Now go! Flee for your life."

Clavius scrambled to his feet, mounted his horse, and rode off.

Rabbi Akiva stood among a small crowd gathered at the outskirts of Temple Mount and watched in awe as the strapping young man single-handedly attacked and overpowered more than a dozen Roman soldiers. He had moved with a lethal grace that could only come from the will of God. That was clear not only by his extraordinary skills but that he had defeated Romans on the holy site. He knew that he had witnessed something very special and was surprised when the man had moved off in the opposite direction, descending from the mount, and quickly disappeared from sight.

The rabbi, who was in his early eighties, active and outgoing, turned to the murmuring crowd and asked: "Who is he? Does anyone know him?"

Everyone fell silent in the presence of the prominent robed rabbi, who was well-known and respected. They shrugged and shook their heads. The rabbi pointed to several men standing close by. "Quickly now. Follow him. Find out everything you can."

The men hurried off. Rabbi Akiva felt a surge of hope for the nascent rebellion that he was supporting. He sensed that the demonstration of power by a single man against a dozen soldiers was an act of God that he was meant to witness. With a man like that on their side, he had no doubt they could overcome great odds and take back their land.

Chapter 3

HADRIAN WAS PERCHED ON HIS luxurious throne in his palace and was visibly upset with the recent turn of events in Judea. If the emperor's stare could kill, Clavius would certainly be dead like all the other soldiers who had died in Jerusalem under the gaze of the statue of Jupiter. A magnificent statue that had been destroyed by one man, who had acted more like Jupiter than all the Roman soldiers in his presence. Considering those events, Hadrian just might condemn the centurion to the death that he'd barely escaped in the province of Judea. Clavius looked at the floor to avoid the emperor's gaze, and nearby General Nepos regarded the centurion with disappointment.

"Just one man, Clavius?" the general asked. "And he was unarmed, is that correct?"

Clavius grimaced for a moment before answering. "Your Majesty, he took us by surprise and disarmed the first soldier he confronted. He was very capable with a sword."

Hadrian didn't think the centurion sounded very convincing. How could one man surprise so many armed soldiers? He wondered if Clavius had begged for his life. "Why did you survive?"

"He wanted me to bring you a message. I've told it to General Nepos."

"Well, I want to hear from you. What is it?"

"He wanted me to tell you that Jerusalem has only one God. But I think he meant the same for all Judea."

"Why do you think that Clavius?" Hadrian asked.

He stared at the floor again. "Because it was the sentiment that I heard wherever we went."

Hadrian frowned at Nepos. Until Clavius had returned to Rome on the orders of General Severus, Nepos had told him that everything was going as planned in Judea and that they were in full control in Judea.

"Who is this man and how did he kill so many people?" Hadrian asked.

"He said his name was Simon ben Kosevah." Clavius looked embarrassed. "We were ambushed, Your Majesty."

"Ambushed by one man. Interesting."

"He was quite extraordinary and…"

Nepos cut in to help Clavius save face. "Yes, he was lucky. A man who just got lucky, Your Majesty."

"I'm sure we'll never encounter him again."

Hadrian thought back to his trip to Judea a year ago. He definitely was not greeted as a savior or a hero. More like an oppressor. But no one had threatened his entourage. He'd met with Rabbi Akiva in Jerusalem and promised him that the people of Judea could continue following their religion. But since then, he'd changed his mind. Religions were devices for rebellion and he was intent on maintaining his empire, if not expanding it. Nothing said that more than the wall he'd built across Britain to protect the Romans from the barbarians of Caledonia.

"And if we do, I trust you will deal with him swiftly, General. And use him as an example of what happens to those who go against Rome. Against me."

Nepos nodded. "Yes, Your Highness."

Hadrian shifted his gaze to Clavius again. "Maybe you've learned a lesson about arrogance, about thinking no one could overpower you." He waited for the centurion to respond.

"Yes, Your Majesty. I won't be fooled again. If you allow me to go back, I will hunt that man down and kill him for you."

Hadrian considered his words. Clavius was an imposing figure because of his size and muscular build. That was the kind of soldier that he wanted in Judea. But he couldn't let him get away without punishment. "I'm removing you as a cohort leader. You are again a single centurion and you will go directly back to Judea and hunt the man who killed your men. Am I understood?"

"Yes, of course, Your Highness. Thank you. Thank you. I appreciate the chance to go back and I will do my best to personally bring this wicked man to justice. We will be ready for him if he dares to show his face again."

Night had fallen in the quaint hillside village of Kuziva. Torches burned in the corners of a courtyard in a modest abode. The sound of stone scraping across steel could be heard as Simon sharpened his sword against a hand-cranked stone. It was the sword he'd taken from the Roman soldier. He held up the sharpened blade and examined it in the torch light.

As he did so, he thought about his battle atop Temple Mount. He was pleased that he'd defeated so many Romans at the temple site that the Romans had destroyed decades earlier. For the first time, it occurred to him that because of the location, he might've been protected by a higher force, the one God. Certainly, that was the way Judea's spiritual leaders would interpret his victory. But he preferred to focus on his skills. After all, he had prepared for such a fight for years. He reviewed the moves he had made while surrounded by six armed men and defeating them without even a scratch.

He knew his master would be proud of him for displaying the expertise and artistry he had been taught. He was only twelve when Master Leon recognized his natural talents and told him that with training and hard work, no one would be able to defeat him in combat. The old man had spent years in Greece studying the art of combat and had learned advanced fighting skills. He had taken on Simon as his only student and turned him into a master warrior.

Before his death, Master Leon had told him that the Roman occupation of Israel was a blessing in disguise for him. He would not have to look hard to find enemies. They would be everywhere. And he would need to learn how to fight multiple enemies at the same time. He had gazed into Simon's eyes and told him: *It will take an entire army to stop you. But you will have your own army to fight them. The people will call upon you. But you are stubborn and will want to avoid what is inevitable.*

Simon's reverie was broken when he heard the sound of footsteps outside the courtyard wall. He moved closer to the entrance and the sound ceased. He listened. Nothing. But he knew someone was there. He slowly turned his sword in hand. "I know you're out there. Show yourself. If I have to come for you, you may very well meet my sword. I've just sharpened it for you."

After a few moments, he heard the crunching footsteps again and this time he knew it was more than one person. If they were coming for him, to kill him or take him into custody, he was ready for them. He wasn't about to give up without a fight. He relaxed at the appearance of an old man garbed in a robe that identified him as a rabbi. Even though he wasn't from Kuziva, Simon recognized him. Behind him, stood a cluster of men, some young, some older.

"You are Simon ben Kosevah, descendant of Yishai from your father's side, and an offspring of the Hasmoneans on your mother's side."

Simon grins, amused. "That is true. So what?"

The rabbi looked stunned. "You have the blood of royalty flowing in your veins – the blood of a ruling dynasty. Yet you live like a commoner."

"To live by other's expectations is just another form of slavery."

"I am Rabbi Akiva."

"I know who you are. But what brings the chief rabbi of Israel to my doorstep?"

The rabbi motioned toward those around him. "We are part of a growing resistance.

We are determined to drive out the Roman occupation. And we could use your help. You impressed us with your fighting skills at Temple Mount."

Simon laughed. "It's just the dozen of you?"

"Another few dozen in the village of Kinneret alongside the sea."

Simon thought of his late master's words again, about how he would try to avoid his destiny. "And what chance do you stand against even one of the many legions of Roman soldiers?"

"A good chance. With your help. We saw how you defeated a dozen soldiers by yourself. You attacked them without a weapon. I thought you were committing suicide in protest of their pagan statue on the site of the holy temple. I was wrong. All of us who watched were wrong."

"I took down a small group of men. There are six thousand men in a Roman legion. And Rome has many legions."

"The only one that concerns us at the moment is the one taking the villages along the Sea of Galilee."

"Why should that concern me?"

The rabbi waved his arm, indicating the entire village. "Simon, your village of Kuziva is in Galilee!"

In spite of what he had been told, Simon shook his head. "But it's far from the sea. It'll take the Romans a while to get here, and I'll be ready for them. I will defend my village but I don't want to join a lost cause."

"Then join us and make it a winning cause," Akiva persisted. "We can win if we work together."

He remembered his master's words and felt the burden of that role. He still wished he could avoid it.

The rabbi shook his head. "I don't understand. You fought those Romans with no concern for your own life."

"I fought alone. I heard what the soldiers were doing in Jerusalem and I wanted to see for myself. I walked for four days and, as it happened, I arrived the day they were raising the pagan statue on the temple site."

"That was no accident," the rabbi attested. "You were guided."

He ignored the comment. "But your small army can't defeat a legion."

"Simon, we have a plan. Would you like to see it?"

He smiled. What did the rabbi know about planning a rebellion against the great Roman military? But he was curious to see how ridiculous the plan must be. "What is it?"

"You will need to come with us to the village of Kinneret."

After a day-long wagon ride to the coast, Simon and Rabbi Akiva strolled along the Kinneret dock after dark with the rabbi's men following. Simon glanced out at the dozens of fishing boats thinking he'd never seen so many boats and wondered if they could be put to use against the Romans.

"What do you think, Simon? Have you been out to sea?"

He could tell that the rabbi was curious about his background. But he wasn't about to chat about his past; the death of his parents, how his uncle had taken him in, then kicked him out, his training in the art of combat. "Never on a boat."

The rabbi stared at Simon, assessing him. "Let's go to our secret meeting place."

The building was a fifteen-minute walk from the dock. The barn door opened and Rabbi Akiva led Simon inside, along with the men who were with him. The interior was lit with torches and there were at least fifty men inside with plenty of room for everyone. They walked over to a man in his forties who was tough-looking and fit. He was studying a large map.

"Simon, this is Noah, our strategist. Noah this is Simon."

Noah glanced at him, nodded dismissively, and then turned back to the map. He pointed at two villages near each other by the sea. "Our sources tell us there are about three hundred Roman soldiers in the villages of Tabgha and Nachum. We have heard that in two days they will leave only a single *centuria* for both villages. That's eighty to a hundred soldiers. The rest of the soldiers will advance on Tiberius."

He tapped on the map at the location of Tiberius, which was much further to the south of the other two villages. "We must not let them take another village. They've already taken the villages on the opposite shore with no opposition. Tomorrow we cross the sea at nightfall and we will set fire to both villages. That disruption should stop the Romans from advancing to Tiberius as they deal with the burning village. We can strike in the dark, killing many Romans before retreating."

Noah regarded the group, but didn't look at Simon, then continued. "Though we are few in numbers, we can defeat them through cunning and strategy."

Heads nodded in agreement and many in the room smiled. But not Simon. "To what end does this strategy gain? You destroy two of your own villages to save only one. And it doesn't really save it. The action merely slows them down."

Noah frowned at him. "We are outnumbered ten to one, or even more. We can't fight them on their own terms. We would be slaughtered."

"But your strategy is simply a distraction. Our goal should be to drive them out of those villages. To do this we need to use deception. We can take those two villages back without raising a sword or a bow."

Noah looked insulted by the insolent newcomer. "Who are you to come in here and—"

Rabbi Akiva raised a hand. "Let's hear him out. Then decide. What are you suggesting, Simon?" Noah looked annoyed but remained silent waiting to hear what Simon had to say.

"Tomorrow morning we should all meet at the dock..." The men listened as Simon spelled out his plan.

Simon stood on the Kinneret dock and guided the rabbi's men as they tied fishing boats together. The day was overcast, but the wind was light and only ripples disturbed the early morning calm of the sea. Simon hoped it stayed that way.

Rabbi Akiva and Noah watched from further down the dock. "You really think this will work?" Noah sounded doubtful and disgruntled that Simon's plan had been adopted over his own.

"He trusts it. And I trust him," the rabbi responded firmly.

Noah shook his head. "I believe you have horse blinders on, dear rabbi."

By midday, Simon was ready to carry out his plan. A light wind created low waves that rocked the boats. The sun had broken through and the puffy white clouds didn't appear to threaten rain. He looked over the boats, which were moored side by side. All the men were gathered behind him. He pivoted to face them.

"It's time. As we discussed, two men were in the boats at each end of the row. Everyone else is to be in the five center-most boats."

The men hurried into the boats, unmoored them, and paddled. As the boats pulled away from the dock, ropes rose from the water between them and pulled tautly, towing the empty boats along with them. The line of boats all moved in unison out to sea.

Clavius and his troops had arrived at the village of Nachum two days earlier, joining two other *centeria,* all part of the legion that had taken over a dozen villages along the Sea of Galilee. He'd no sooner made camp on the outskirts of the village when his new commander, a centurion who had taken over his role following his demotion, rode up and dismounted. "Centurion Clavius," he said smugly, barely hiding a grin. "You and your troops will remain here to hold Nachum. The rest of us will leave in the morning."

"Why is that?"

"Are you questioning my authority?"

"Of course not. You are just following orders," Clavius said, deflating the man's newfound sense of superiority.

He nodded. "We have more villages to take. We'd headed for Tiberius."

"Good luck."

The departure of two *centuria* seemed to have little if any effect on the villagers who mostly remained in their homes and shops. The village leader, an old bearded man had come to camp and given Clavius a loaf of bread. He had accepted it, but he didn't think it was an offer of friendship. "We are running low on supplies and need to know if farmers will be allowed to bring their harvest to the market without it being stolen."

Clavius said he would order his soldiers not to take anything from the carts entering the village unless they contained weapons. In that case, the penalties would be severe. The old man had no sooner left when a soldier rushed up to Clavius.

"Sir, you must come to the dock. A row of boats on the sea is heading this way."

Clavius and a dozen other mounted soldiers rode to the sea and observed the approaching vessels. Rumors about a rebellion had reached the troops and Clavius realized that he might be facing an invading army. He stared out to sea and counted the boats. "They must know that most of the troops have left," he said to the soldier next to him. "With the likelihood of more boats beyond the ones we see, there could be…" He hesitated. "At least a hundred."

"Yes, sir. And with five or more men to each boat…"

"We could be outnumbered five to one or more," Clavius said.

The soldiers on horseback formed a circle around him as he pondered the situation. They kept glancing out to sea with uneasy looks. Clavius knew he would be a hero if his men held off an attack from the sea against overwhelming odds. But if they were slaughtered, he might as well be one of the dead because Emperor Hadrian and General Nepos would see him as a twice-failed leader losing his soldiers to a weaker force.

Clavius made up his mind. "We evacuate the village."

He tugged on the reins of his horse, shifting directions. They quickly grabbed what they could from their encampment, leaving behind foodstuff and gear, and within minutes mounted their horses and abandoned the village. Clavius circled back to make sure no one was left behind. As he rode away, villagers peaked out of their houses and gawked at the departing soldiers. There were no doubt as they hoped they were gone for good and never to return.

Chapter 4

SIMON'S FIRST BOAT RIDE WAS an extraordinary experience that he would never forget. In spite of his initial uneasiness when his boat started rocking as the wind picked up, he kept his gaze on the distant horizon watching for land. After all, he had created a rebellion 'navy,' and he was determined to ride it out like a sailor on high sea. He and the other four in his boat had taken turns paddling as the line of mostly empty boats moved slowly across the Sea of Galilee toward Nachum.

Now as they reached the village, Simon leaped onto the dock with his sword ready. Half a dozen others quickly joined him, ready to engage the enemy. They couldn't see any Roman soldiers, but he knew they might be hiding, waiting in ambush. Once the boats were all moored, Simon led them forward and they proceeded cautiously to shore, swords drawn. They no sooner touched land when several men rushed out to confront them. Simon tensed, then was relieved to see that they were unarmed villagers.

Rabbi Akiva stepped ashore and villagers appeared from around corners and gazed out through windows and doorways when they saw the rabbi coming toward them. They quickly came out from hiding, rushed to their rescuers, and surrounded the rabbi and Simon.

"The Romans?" Akiva asked.

The villagers joyously shook their heads, smiled, and motioned in the direction they'd fled. "The Romans rode off very fast on their horses after they saw all the boats coming," a teenage boy shouted.

The rabbi patted Simon on the back. "It worked! We did it."

Simon was pleased, but he knew it was a minor victory. "We won by deception. But the truth is that my small band of men cannot overcome an entire legion of Roman soldiers."

Simon noticed that Noah grimaced when he'd heard him refer to the raiding party as *his* band. But he also saw Rabbi Akiva nod in agreement to everything he was saying. His men gathered around him and he realized they were waiting for new orders. They had accepted him as their leader. But he had no idea what they would do next. Except they needed to expand their fighting force and to do it quickly. He hoped they could find new recruits from the village before they moved on.

"Let's set up camp and see what the Romans left behind. Tonight, we'll revel in our victory, no matter how small," Simon told his men. "Then tomorrow we'll move on."

That evening, the village erupted in a spontaneous and raucous celebration as the residents of the Nachum and the entire rebellion force turned out in the village square. Musicians played on their instruments and Simon recognized a psaltery, zither, dulcimer, and a lute. Some of the musicians, he was told, came from the neighboring village of Tabgha and he was told that it was also abandoned by Roman troops in the wake of the fleeing soldiers from Nachum. That was good news. A double victory!

Following Rabbi Akiva's suggestion, Simon mounted a horse and watched from the edge of the plaza. The rabbi strode to the center of the merriment and called for everyone's attention. "I want to present the man who made this all possible."

With that, Simon rode into their midst.

"Simon ben Kosevah!" Akiva shouted.

Everyone cheered but Simon couldn't help but notice that Noah looked on silently, no doubt jealous of his success. He also probably knew that the rabbi had set up this presentation. Simon focused on the crowd and spoke in a commanding voice that immediately compelled everyone to listen.

"Your village is just the beginning! We will take back Israel, one village at a time if we must, but we will take it back! All of it! We will expel Rome and their pagan gods with them! We will give all of Israel back to our God! Our one true God!"

The crowd cheered, drunk on the ecstasy of the moment. "But my small band of men cannot do this alone! We need all able-bodied men! Judeans, Samaritans, everyone."

The mention of Samaritans triggered some boos from the crowd of villagers and soldiers. "We can't trust them," Noah shouted.

"No! Everyone is welcome! Christians too! Everyone! We are not the only ones in Israel who want the Romans out."

The crowd went silent for a moment or two, and then suddenly burst into a frenzy of cheers. Simon spreads his arms wide, oozing charisma and Rabbi Akiva looks on in childlike wonder.

Villagers and would-be warriors danced and drank, and the young women couldn't take their gaze off Simon as they whispered among themselves. Simon watched from the sidelines and clapped for the musicians, but remained comparatively subdued. He knew the others were watching him to see if he would get drunk, dance wantonly, and pursue the young women.

But he wanted to keep his men focused on the task ahead and not give into momentary pleasures that might make them rethink their commitment to the rebellion. If he was going to do this, it would require complete commitment. Half-way was not acceptable and he wanted his men to understand that. After all, he knew this was just the beginning, definitely not the end. Finally, an older woman approached Simon, took his arm, and pointed at the younger women in sight. "See those girls. I'm sure any one of them would like to dance with you."

"They are all lovely, but I have two left feet and I don't want to step on theirs. So I will just watch and express my joy quietly."

Later, when the celebration had settled down, Simon sat by a fire enjoying deer meat and wine with Rabbi Akiva when two men in their mid-twenties approached their table. Simon had seen them talking with several men from his band, who were laughing as they boasted about their deceptive attack on the Romans. The two men had eagerly listened and glanced over in his direction a couple of times as they heard the story. Simon figured they would make good additions to their band if they were committed to the cause, and now here they were.

One was tall and lanky, the other a few inches shorter, broad-chested, and muscular. Both had short-cropped hair and rosy cheeks, probably from too much wine. "Sorry to bother you," the taller of the two began. My name is Levi and my friend here is Rubin. Rabbi Akiva, Master Simon, we are honored to be in your presence."

"And I am honored to be here," Simon interjected.

"We would like to have a few words with you."

The rabbi smiled. "Sit down you two. What do you have to say for yourselves?"

They quickly took seats, then looked between each other and Rubin said, "You go, Levi."

The young villager leaned forward. "We have some important information for you. Something secret."

"Go on," Rabbi Akiva said. "What is it?"

"We are part of an underground Judean patriots. We have been preparing in the villages on this coast for a rebellion for some time, in fact, for years. We've been gathering arms and fortifying some caves that can serve as subterranean passages. We are all with you. Give the word and we will join your cause."

"How many are you?"

"At least fifty, maybe more, are ready and willing. But we're sure there are hundreds more in the villages on the sea who will join if they see there's any chance of defeating the Romans."

Simon wolfishly smiled and took a bite of deer meat as he watched Rubin and Levi gleefully wander back to the celebration. "Next, we take back Jerusalem."

Rabbi Akiva looked stunned. "Do you really think we're ready?"

"Do you think Rome expects us?" Simon countered. "We'll take them by surprise. Just like we did here. Now is the time. While they are unprepared."

He took another bite of deer meat and thought about how his master had taught him to fight more than one man at a time and how he had expanded that idea to how a small army could overcome a larger one. Skill and motivation were key but there was something else too. Destiny. At the time, he didn't understand what Master Leon was talking about. But he understood it now. He felt it running through his blood and he knew it was the time to act.

Hadrian didn't like what he was hearing. Not a bit. He sat on his throne in the Great Hall staring at General Nepos, whose forehead was dappled with perspiration. "Four villages along the Galilee have fallen, General? That land now belongs to Rome. And I intend to take it back."

Hadrian stood up and paced. He used to be able to find solace with Antinous when things didn't go as he expected. It wasn't the same with the empress. She looked at events through her own eyes and how they affected her as an empress. When they didn't go as she wished, she wasn't exactly sympathetic.

"How is this even possible? The Judeans have no real military capabilities. How many Roman soldiers were killed?"

"I don't know, Your Majesty. It's confusing. They attacked from the sea with an overwhelming force, and…"

"What? Are you saying our troops fled? They didn't fight?"

Perspiration was dripping down Nepos' cheeks, which had turned red. "There was only one centuria left behind in the two villages and they were caught off guard. So the centurion at Nachum thought it best to abandon the village, and the others did the same as they left."

"Disgraceful! An embarrassment. What if word of this reaches other provinces?"

"The other provinces are fully under our control." Nepos patted the air with his hands in a gesture to calm the emperor, but it wasn't working. "It's just a minor rebellion that will be quashed, Your Majesty. Their victories are temporary. I assure you."

Hadrian wasn't in his position as emperor by ignoring troubling developments. In this case, there was a particular concern that nagged at him. "Tell me, Nepos, do you think this man – Simon ben Kosevah – is behind the Judean rebellion of the villages?

"I don't know, Your Majesty. We are hunting him and if he shows his face we will close in and capture or kill him."

Hadrian gave Nepos a hard stare. "Find people that know him. Make them talk. He must have friends and a family. Where is he from?"

Nepos swallowed and looked uneasy. "We still don't know. But I believe it is one of the villages in Galilee."

Hadrian shook his head in disgust. "Is Jerusalem secure?"

"Yes. Jerusalem has at least a thousand seasoned soldiers holding it. Nothing will happen there."

"Be sure you keep it that way."

"Yes, my emperor."

"You're dismissed." Hadrian watched Nepos walk away. He had a bad feeling about the Judeans. He made a fist and pounded it into his palm. What audacity. How had they managed to drive the troops out? Simon ben Kosevah. That name came to mind again. He must be involved somehow.

Hadrian let out a sigh. He had plans for a journey north to view the construction of his wall in Britain. He wanted to encourage the local people to join the soldiers in the work. He would tell them that the wall was for their own safety; to protect them from the barbarians to the north. Everything was ready for his journey. But now he didn't feel good about leaving Rome and losing contact with events in Israel. He feared if he were out of touch, the situation would just get worse. Besides, he had yet to find a companion worthy of replacing Antinous. The ones he'd considered only reminded him of how much he missed Antinous. Beyond that, Sabina had told him that she had other plans and wouldn't join him on the journey.

He snapped his fingers and Linus, his chief assistant, emerged from a portico to the side where he'd been waiting discreetly. He trusted the older man, whose gray beard reminded Hadrian of the Greek philosophers. Linus, in fact, had been one of Hadrian's childhood teachers and had accompanied Hadrian on trips to Greece. He knew that Linus was looking forward to the journey to Britain, a province that he'd never visited. But that wasn't going to happen. "Cancel the trip, Linus. I'm staying in Rome for now." He didn't need to explain. Linus had heard his conversation with Nepos.

He blinked, then nodded. "Yes, Your Majesty."

Chapter 5

SIMON AND NOAH WENT ABOUT organizing the troops into groups of fifty soldiers each. Altogether, there were twenty groups, nearly a thousand soldiers and more were arriving regularly at their hidden encampment. But after weeks of training, Simon was anxious to mobilize the troops and attack Jerusalem before the Romans discovered their base. It was time for action. He inspected each group and selected two soldiers as officers in each, one as the lead officer and a backup. In the coming siege, the soldiers would stay with their group as long as possible.

Their encampment, located on the foothills of Mount Nebo, wasn't the best place for either their camp or for training new soldiers because of the rugged terrain. But it was hidden away from the Romans. Rabbi Akiva had selected the site and he defended it at every possible chance because the alternate location, Masada, was one that he found abhorrent. He also pointed out that it would take two days to reach Jerusalem from either site.

As they'd gathered more recruits from the villages along the Sea of Galilee, Simon realized they needed a base to train the newcomers and prepare for their attack. Rabbi Palmer, a corpulent man who hid his bulk under his robe, had suggested they go to Masada on the Dead Sea where a fortress already existed on a flat mountaintop. But the very idea had enraged Rabbi Akiva. He'd told Palmer, Simon and Noah, and the other rabbis that Masada was a sacred site where Israelis had died sixty-five years ago at the end of their last rebellion against the Romans.

Unlike everyone else present, Akiva had been alive at the time, a young teenager who had lived through the Roman siege of Jerusalem. The surviving troops had fled to Masada to join other rebels. A total of 960 rebels lived at Masada until they were attacked by 8,000 Roman soldiers who surrounded and overcame the mountain base. Everyone, except for two women and five children, committed suicide rather than becoming Roman slaves. Masada had remained uninhabited since that time.

Simon stepped up onto a platform to address the troops. A hush fell over the soldiers and all eyes were on Simon. "The day has come," he shouted. "Are you ready?"

The troops responded with cheers. He nodded. "We will attack Jerusalem at dawn and catch the Romans by surprise. It will be the most significant battle of our rebellion. We will take back Jerusalem. Do you hear me?" He raised his voice, shouting:" We will take back our holy capital and drive out the Romans."

The troops cheered wildly and began chanting his name over and over again. After half a minute, Simon raised his hands and patted the air quieting the troops again. "I will lead the way into the city and into the victory. But I need all of you to help. You've been trained to fight and to kill. That is your mission. Do not hesitate or you will be killed."

More shouts and cheers and chanting followed until Simon again quieted the troops. "Every one of you has lived your entire live under the rule of the Roman oppressors. But we are going to change that. We will live for the first time in our lives as free people."

"Let's go!" someone yelled.

Simon laughed. "It won't be long. But you must go into the fight with knowledge of your history. Jerusalem was taken down by Rome sixty-five years ago. The terrible fifth and twelfth legions were the ones who destroyed our capital in that first rebellion. Now, we are ready to confront troops from those same legions which have occupied the city ever since."

He didn't know if that was true, that soldiers from the fifth and twelfth were still in Jerusalem. But it gave his troops additional motivation to attack and kill. "The good news is that the Romans feel so in control of Jerusalem that they have left only about one thousand troops in the city. We can handle them. We can destroy them the way they destroyed our capital." He finished by telling them to eat, rest, and sleep, and be ready to be awakened in the middle of the night to ride like the wind.

The thunderous pounding of hoofs banished Simon's fatigue and filled him with energy as he and his small army charged across the desert toward Jerusalem. He had underestimated the willingness of Judeans to join his cause. But his name had spread among the villages and he was heralded as the Israeli hope for freedom. Master Leon had foretold his path and now he was fully committed. Hundreds of men on horseback made up his army, a ragtag group of farmers, merchants, craftsmen, and others. Some were armed with swords, others with makeshift weapons made from farm tools.

They reached the outskirts of the city and Simon was prepared for a bloodbath. He doubted that the Roman soldiers would flee as they'd done in the villages along the Galilee. A few Roman soldiers outside the city were caught off guard and desperately attempted to hold their ground against the oncoming stampede. They drew their weapons and faced the onslaught.

The thought of engaging the soldiers filled Simon with bloodlust. "Take no prisoners!" he shouted.

He led the way directly at the soldiers, separating himself from the pack. Two soldiers charged toward him, approaching from either side, their swords raised. At the last moment, Simon cut to his left in front of one of the horses, which reared up throwing the rider to the ground. Simon pulled up short, turning his horse back, and slashed the throat of the fallen soldier.

The other one came around behind Simon and swept his sword at him. But Simon swung his sword in a backhand motion blocking the

Roman's swing and the shriek of metal against metal rang out. Simon came in closer so the two horses were side by side and the soldier couldn't swing or stab with his sword. In a single swift motion, Simon pulled out his knife, stabbed him in the gut, and shoved him off his horse.

All around him, Simon's soldiers battled the remaining Romans posted outside the city. Simon galloped ahead, caught up to the pack, and led his surging army into Jerusalem. Roman soldiers patrolling the market and streets were caught by surprise as they attempted to organize a defense. With the suddenness and swiftness of a roaring flood, Simon's expanded band flowed into the street, cutting down the Romans. They were quickly bolstered by residents who joined in the fray, jerking Roman soldiers off their horses and stomping on them, and battering them with any objects they could find.

When it became clear that his men were dominating the battle and the Romans were floundering, Simon rode to the edge of the deadly ruckus and was joined by Rabbi Akiva and Noah. The three looked on at the mayhem, and Simon felt proud of his army. "Not too long ago we were fifty, today we are hundreds, tomorrow we will be thousands."

Noah nodded. "How long before Rome knows what happened here?"

"If no soldiers escaped, then possibly weeks," Akiva estimated.

"Enough time for us to do what must be done," Simon said.

"Which is?" Akiva asked.

Simon didn't answer. He was lost in the rapture of the massacre and was amazed to see women joining the men with sticks and earthenware pots and pans thrashing and beating fallen Romans. Clearly, the people of Jerusalem had enough of the occupation.

At mid-morning the next day Simon stood on a raised platform near the market and looked over the thousands who had gathered to hear him speak. *All these people staring at me.* He felt nervous about addressing such a large crowd. He'd never done anything like it in his young life.

They must realize, he thought, that the Romans will return with reinforcements. He didn't know much about the Roman emperor, but he was certain that Hadrian would not allow Israel to fall without a fight. Finally, he stepped forward to the edge of the platform and called out in a loud voice. "The battle is over."

Cheers answered him.

"We have expelled the Romans. We defeated soldiers from the fifth and the twelfth legions, the ones that destroyed the Holy Temple sixty-five years ago. We have captured our sacred capital – Jerusalem – and freed our country. Israel is the only country in the entire Roman Empire to gain independence. This is a great victory. Today, we stand as free men in our own country, having the right to raise arms and fight for our freedom. That is victory in itself."

More cheers.

"We control Jerusalem again. Now let's fortify the city. Let's make it impossible for them to ever take it back."

The cheering intensified.

"Down with Rome! Down with Rome!"

Uproarious cheers greet Simon's comments and he basked in the glory. He heard shouts: "Long live Simon! Long live Simon! Simon our leader!"

He took it all in absorbing the energy, the power of leadership. Now he knew what it felt like to be not only a leader of a rebellion but a leader of the people. "This city belongs to us, not the Romans, not Hadrian. We will tear down their statues and build a massive wall around the city. We will repair the damaged buildings. And we will build an altar on the Temple Mount."

The cheers that erupted were even louder and then the entire crowd chanted in unison: "Simon! Simon! Simon!"

He took in a deep breath, exhaled, smiled, and waved. There was now no doubt he was the leader of Israel. But he couldn't help wondering: How could he have arisen so quickly from an unknown young man in a small village to a military leader, a national hero? How did it happen? And where will it end? Master Leon never told him the final outcome. That was for him to discover.

Ruth stood near the front of the crowd and stared up in wide-eyed admiration at Simon on the platform. She'd never seen such a handsome, vibrant young man. He was tall, muscular and exuded charisma that captivated everyone in the crowd. He seemed larger than life, and what astonishing stories she'd heard about him. Maybe he *was* larger than life.

Her friend, Mary, standing next to her, clasped her arm. "Ruth, you look like you've seen God!"

"Stop, Mary. He's a man."

"Yes, but what a man!"

"Look, he's coming."

Simon climbed down from the platform and moved through the crowd. Ruth's heart fluttered as he moved in her direction. Their eyes met, he smiled, lingered a moment, then moved on. She was spellbound and hoped that he was attracted by her good looks and long flowing raven hair. She'd been told many times that she was strikingly beautiful and slowly she had come to accept it as true, even though she always had doubts about herself and how she fit into this world.

She caught her breath, hardly believing what just happened. Mary shook her arm snapping her out of her trance. "Ruth, he stopped right in front of you! And I could tell he liked what he saw!"

"Do you think so? I'm just pleased that he actually looked at me."

Simon wore a cloth that covered his nose and mouth, which was tied behind his head. He was supervising the burning of Roman soldiers.

Their weapons and protective gear were removed and placed in a separate pile from the heap of tangled bodies. He didn't allow himself to feel any sympathy for the young fallen soldiers whose bloodied bodies laid on the massive funeral pyre. They'd come to his country unwanted. They were invaders. In a rebellion, death always awaits. Better that it be the enemy. Their sacrifices empowered Simon and his growing army, making him and his followers feel unbeatable. The more Roman soldiers that fell to his sword and to the weapons of his loyal troops the better.

"Burn them!" Simon ordered.

"But there are still more to come," replied one of the soldiers who had just tossed a body onto the pile.

"Then we'll burn more tomorrow." He turned to Noah. "Distribute the weapons, armor and shields to our soldiers who need them."

"Yes, sir. But there's something I want to tell you."

Simon stared hard at Noah. He was well aware that until they'd taken Jerusalem, Noah had only grudgingly accepted Simon as their leader. But something had changed with this victory. What is it, Noah?"

"I want you to know that I will continue to question your decisions when I don't agree with them. That said, you should know that I admire your leadership and your incredible fighting abilities." Noah dropped to one knee and looked up at Simon. "I hereby pledge my allegiance to you no matter what will come, and I am ready to die for you."

"Thank you, Noah. Stand up. I appreciate that but I don't want you to die. I want to live and I want to hear your advice even, especially when you don't agree with me. I hereby appoint you as my chief advisor and as a general in the Judean Rebel Army."

"I am very grateful, My Lord." Noah raised his gaze and looked over Simon's shoulder. "Oh, I forgot."

"What is it?"

Noah motioned to Rubin and Levi, who had joined Simon's band in the village of Nachum, and they dragged heavy bags over to Simon.

They emptied the contents, mounds of coins. "Roman coins found in the garrison encampment," Noah explained.

Simon picked up one of the coins and rolled it between his fingers, studying the Roman symbols on it as well as Hadrian's image. "These now belong to us. But let's make them ours. Over-stamp them."

"With what, sir?" Noah asked.

Simon's features slowly shifted into a grin as he worked through his thoughts. "The Holy Temple with the Ark of the Covenant within. It will represent my promise to rebuild the temple. Include the inscription, "To the freedom of Jerusalem." Simon paused, seeing the coin in his mind's eye, then continued. "And on the other side, my name is Simon, President of Israel."

"Yes, sir." Noah looked at Levi and Rubin. "We will find a master engraver and silver smith. They will re-make these coins and make them truly ours."

"Good. One other thing, Noah. Get the best of our soldiers ready for action tomorrow."

Noah looked stunned. "Could I ask what you have in mind?"

Simon smiled. "Of course. We're going to go about the city and destroy every last statue that the Romans erected here. We are going to erase them from the face of the city."

"With pleasure, sir."

Ruth looked out the small window of her small mud brick home on the outskirts of Jerusalem and watched the activity on the street as she brushed her hair. Her best friend, Mary, relaxed on Ruth's bed, waiting for her to finish getting ready to go out. Ruth put the brush down and picked up her hand mirror, briefly studied herself, then put the mirror face-down on the small table in her room. She appreciated the mirror made of polished metal, a gift from her father when she was a child. But she believed that spending too much time gazing into a mirror meant a woman was weak in character. Besides, she would rather look at other people than at herself.

"I'm ready, I guess." She and Mary left the house and headed for the market. Ruth wasn't interested in shopping as much as finding out more about Simon and, if they were lucky, seeing him. Of course, she would not try to approach him. She was not that kind of woman. She would simply watch from a distance.

Mary, her friend since childhood, knew her well and read her thoughts. "You're thinking about him, aren't you?"

"Who are you talking about?"

"You know who," Mary answered with a laugh.

"He liberated us."

"Yes. Him and his army."

"But he is their leader."

"You are very taken with him."

Ruth blushed. "He's so handsome and strong, who wouldn't be?"

"Yes, handsome and strong," she answered in a teasing voice. "Maybe someday he'll marry you. Mary beamed at her and Ruth turned a bright red. "That's what you're thinking. Admit it."

Ruth shrugged. "It's just a wild dream that will never happen. After all, Simon can have any woman he desires." Ruth gazed off into the distance, her eyes full of hope despite her words.

They continued walking and it didn't take long before they heard bits of gossip that Simon and some of his soldiers were riding throughout the city tearing down the Roman statues. Ruth felt a thrill at the thought of the muscular Simon pulling down statues. She glanced at Mary. "There's that stupid statue of the naked man or god or whatever by the market. Let's go see if they've destroyed it."

"That's Apollo. He's a Greek god and a Roman god."

"How do you know that?" Ruth asked, curiously.

"I was in the market when a Roman officer called everyone over for the dedication. He said Apollo was a healer and a prophet, god of music and poetry."

"What did everyone think of that?" Ruth asked.

"Not much. Nobody said anything. Except for one kid who yelled, 'Where's his pants?' and everyone laughed and walked away."

"Oh, look! Is that blood?" Ruth pointed at small red pools and dark brown stains on the street. She and Mary had smartly avoided going out during the battle for Jerusalem or in the aftermath when slain bodies were piled on the street. Ruth covered her face at the acrid smell of ashes and they passed a few paces from a smoldering pile that she realized must be human remains now charred bones and cinders.

"Keep walking," Mary said.

A couple of minutes later, the market came into view. "Oh, look, the statue. It's still there."

Mary laughed. "You sound happy about that."

"Mary, why would you say that?" She was right, of course. It meant Simon and the soldiers hadn't gotten there yet.

Before Mary could answer, the thunder of galloping horses caught their attention and they quickly moved to the side of the street. Soldiers charged past and Ruth momentarily glimpsed Simon leading the way. "Let's hurry. I want to watch."

Ruth caught her breath as they got closer and saw Simon approach the tall statue on his horse. She thought he would pull it down and do it with ease. She'd heard about how he had pulled down the twenty-foot-tall statue of Jupiter from the Temple Mount after he single-handedly defeated all the Romans there. But that wasn't what he did. Instead, he withdrew his sword and decapitated Apollo with one swift swing. He moved aside and the other soldiers took turns hacking at the statue, cutting off arms, then legs, and it toppled over. But they weren't finished. They continued taking turns chopping up the statue until all that was left was a pile of rubble.

Simon and the soldiers had fire in their eyes and unbridled anger in their swings. They weren't just demolishing statues. They were assaulting the very beliefs in the gods that the statue represented, the belief that had been forced upon them by the Romans.

Simon trotted toward the market where hundreds were now gathered. Ruth and Mary had blended into the crowd. Ruth was at once fascinated but also somewhat frightened at what she'd seen. Simon was still fighting the Romans and all that the statues represented. His entire being was infused with anger during his assault on Apollo. He had destroyed the last representatives of the occupiers.

"Citizens of Jerusalem. No more! No more! The Romans are defeated. Their statues destroyed!"

A cheer rose. "No more! No more!" the crowd answered. Simon's fellow soldiers, including Noah, Levi, and Rubin, had lined up on their horses next to him.

Simon smiled and nodded in agreement. His gaze swept across the crowd and Ruth thought that for a moment he had looked right at her again. But she was probably imagining it.

"Come to Temple Mount tomorrow. I will talk to all in Jerusalem. I want everyone to be there. It will be important. So, tell all of your friends. Spread the word."

With that, Simon and the soldiers rode off.

Chapter 6

Less than an hour had passed since the carpenters had finished constructing a platform atop Temple Mount and an altar. And already a massive crowd had gathered and more and more were showing up. From where he stood off to one side of the stage, it seemed that every resident of Jerusalem was congregating on the side of Temple Mount and beyond.

He smiled as Levi walked up to him. "Can you believe all these people? Look how far the crowd goes."

"The people of Jerusalem are curious to see and hear their mysterious new leader who miraculously defeated the Roman legion and freed Jerusalem."

"But how will they be able to hear me?"

"That's what I want to talk to you about. You need to speak only a few words at a time, then pause. We have placed people throughout the crowd who will repeat your words. And others farther back will repeat their words so that everyone hears what you say."

Simon considered the plan, then laughed. "I can do that. I just hope that when my words reach the people farthest back that they are the same ones I said. I'll shout my words, though, so at least some of the people can hear them directly from me."

Levi moved away and Rabbi Akiva stepped forward bearing a purple robe. "It's time, Simon. Please wear this robe. You want to show your status to your people." He nodded somewhat reluctantly. He knew what was coming.

After he donned the robe, Simon saw who had accompanied Akiva to the Temple Mount.

"Simon, I have someone who would like to meet you. This is…"

"Rabbi Elazar Hamuda," Simon said. Not the person he wanted standing by him at this crucial moment when he would make an important proclamation.

Akiva was taken aback that Simon already knew Elazar.

"He is my nephew," Elazar said.

"On my mother's side," Simon added. Akiva noticed the tension between him and Elazar but he ignored it. Simon had lived with Elazar for a few months after his parents died in a fire that destroyed their home. Elazar was strict with him and he rebelled by breaking a cherished ceramic pot. Elazar accused Simon of starting the fire that killed his parents, kicked him out of the house, and told him never to return. Fortunately, an old Greek man who had lived in the village for a few years took him in and Simon became his student in the martial arts.

"I would like to make an announcement to the crowd," Akiva said, interrupting Simon's reverie.

Simon glanced at Elazar, a slender elderly who stood by piously, hands folded in front of him. Then back to Akiva. "Yes, but after me," Simon responded.

The rabbi nodded in agreement, and Simon stepped forward on the platform in his new royal garb. He shrugged off his annoyance at the arrival of Elazar. Instantly, applause and cheers rippled through the crowd starting from near the platform and flowing outward to the far reaches of his audience.

Rubin and Levi stood proudly nearby. He'd met the two soldiers at the celebration in Nachum, and they had become his closest allies and protectors. Initially, Simon wasn't comfortable with the idea of two men accompanying him like dogs everywhere he went. He knew it was Rabbi

Akiva's doing, but he still ignored them and told them he didn't need their help. Yet they continued to faithfully wait outside of his tent in the army's encampment and closely followed him when he left.

He'd finally conceded that as Israeli's leader, he must accept that he would always have an entourage of advisors and protectors. He grudgingly accepted that new way of living as a necessity, and fortunately, he liked the two men who were just a couple years younger than him. And that wasn't the only matter that Rabbi Akiva had convinced Simon to accept. He and the rabbi were about to reveal another one of far more significance.

He stared out not moving or speaking and gradually the clapping faded as the huge crowd waited to hear him speak. The sun was just setting and many in the massive crowd held torches. He turned his focus to those nearest him in the crowd. He could see their faces, their eyes, their expressions. His gaze fell on a young woman he was sure that he'd seen in the crowd when he spoke after the Romans were defeated. She was astonishingly beautiful with long dark hair that glistened in the torchlight. She was staring at him, wide-eyed, and at that moment, he knew he needed to meet her. He smiled and spread his arms as if welcoming the massive audience. "We are standing on sacred ground." He paused and heard his words repeated through the crowd. "The holy temple existed here for a thousand years." He spoke with a booming voice and wondered how many people could actually hear him. At least they could hear his words repeated, if not directly from him. "It was the light of Israel… the most sacred place."

His words had become a massive echo. It seemed more and more people were shouting his words, not just the ones assigned to do so. That was unexpected and a bit hilarious. "We have taken back what rightfully belongs to us… I swear that on this site…we will rebuild our third Holy Temple… our everlasting temple…for the new generations to come…or I will die trying!" His words reverberated and it sounded as if everyone was saying that they would die trying.

"Who is with me?"

Once everyone has heard the question, the crowd shouted back, "We are! We are!"

Then Simon shouted again, "Who is with me?"

His echoed words are followed by the same response, "We are! We are!" And they continued repeating it.

Simon yelled back to the crowd, "Freedom or death! Do not fear the Romans… you can put your trust in me… I am assuming the title of *N'si Yisrael* – The Prince of Israel!"

He studied the surprised expressions on the faces closest to him in the crowd. "For I have been sent to you and all the Judeans from heaven!"

The crowd erupted in cheers. Rabbi Akiva moved next to Simon as Levi and Rubin took a couple steps back. Akiva smiled with satisfaction. But Simon couldn't help noticing that his uncle, Elazar, looked mortified. Other rabbis, who stood off to the side, looked confused.

Simon locked his gaze onto the young woman who was staring at him with intense admiration. He didn't know her. Never had spoken to her. Yet, he felt attracted to her like to no other woman. His master had urged him not to get distracted by girls, if he wanted to achieve the highest level of the Spartan martial arts. Doing so would delude his attention and energy, and might even cause him to abandon his quest to gain the ultimate powers; powers that would allow him to become unbeatable against great odds. But now, he felt a desire for a woman in his life. Not any woman, certainly not a wonton one, but this one. He somehow knew their attraction to each other was mutual. Simon glanced over to Levi and motioned him over as the crowd continued to cheer and call out his name.

"That woman in front, with the long black hair."

"Yes, My Lord, I see her."

It was the first time Levi or anyone had addressed him formally. "Find out who she is and where she lives."

"Yes, sir," he replied and hurried off.

As the cheers faded, Rabbi Akiva triumphantly stepped forward holding a Torah scroll. He and Simon faced each other in front of the altar. "Simon Ben Kosevah, as the chief rabbi and spiritual leader of Israel, I give you my blessing, and declare your new surname as Bar Kochva, meaning "Son of Star," for I announce to all that you are the messiah, the one that we have been waiting for.

Holding up the Torah scroll, he said, "Let me read from Numbers 24:17,19: *A star will come out of Jacob; a scepter will rise out of Israel… a ruler will come out of Jacob.*"

Again, the crowd erupted and raised the cheers to an even higher level. Simon glanced at his uncle and saw that Elazar was stone-faced, no doubt appalled. When the cheering finally started to fade, Simon turned to Akiva. "Thank you. They seem to accept me."

Akiva patted him on the back. "Of course, they accept you. Did you hear them?"

"Yes, but we have no time for celebration. We must gather as many men as we can and prepare to free more villages from Roman occupation as soon as possible. This will keep the Romans off-guard and allow us to continue building our army as we move from village to village. We will start with Eilabun. It's the closest, and we can be there before the soldiers are aware an attack is on the way."

Akiva nodded. "It will be done. You are a military genius as well as the long-awaited messiah."

"And you are a great strategist who can see the larger picture."

Chapter 7

Clavius sat at a table under the shade of a tree in the town square drinking tea with two other centurions. They'd spent weeks in the village of Eilabun, awaiting the arrival of replacement troops and new orders from General Severus. With six hundred soldiers, the village on the northern side of the Sea of Galilee was secure, much more so than other villages on this coast when only one centuria was present. That had been a tactical mistake, but at the time, the Romans were unaware that a small underground rebellion had fomented into action. He couldn't help wondering what was going on in Jerusalem. He'd heard rumors about the rebels planning an attack on the capital but he doubted that their untrained soldiers could take the capital, even if their numbers had increased over the past few months. He knew that Hadrian would send more troops if the threat was real.

Clavius raised a hand and a woman appeared moments later from one of the shops. "That was faster than usual," he remarked to the other centurions who laughed. He looked at the unsmiling middle-aged woman and asked for more biscuits. She nodded and moved off. The villagers were subdued but obedient. All it took was a couple of hangings of young rabble-rousers and the village was pacified.

One of the other centurions complained about being stuck there and wanted to go back to Rome and be reassigned to another province. Clavius nodded in agreement. More than anything, he would like to return to the capital and see his family. But not if it meant that Hadrian would order his execution. As far as he knew, none of the generals had complained to the emperor about how he abandoned the Nachum. Otherwise, he would've been recalled again and surely faced deadly consequences. It actually seemed that General Severus liked him. But again, it was probably that he was impressed by his size and brawn.

A soldier rode up on his horse and Clavius could immediately tell that something new was finally happening. Hopefully, more troops were arriving with new orders for them to return to Rome. But he knew that part was a faint hope. Hadrian wanted more troops in Israel, not less. "What is it, soldier?"

"The rebels are coming. It's Simon and his little army."

All three centurions bolted from the table and pulled out their swords. "Alert everyone," Clavius shouted at the rider as they rushed to their horses. Within minutes, hundreds of Romans were gathered on horseback at the encampment outside of the village. A distant cloud of dust was visible and rolling in their direction. From the size of the cloud, it looked as if Simon had as many troops as they did. But he wasn't about to be fooled again. He'd belatedly learned from an Israeli spy that that most of the boats attacking Nachum had been empty.

The captain of the cohort, a centurion named Felix, who had taken over Clavius's position after he was demoted, called everyone's attention. "We'll engage them in the open fields!" he shouted. Moments later, the five centuria of soldiers charged away from the village.

"Why fight them out here if they've got superior numbers?" one of the other centurions called out to him as they rode away.

Clavius looked over at him and laughed. "Maybe because Felix thinks it's easier to escape; better than being trapped in the village."

Once they had spotted Eilabun in the distance across the desert, Simon picked up the pace and led his ragtag rebels at blinding speed toward the village and the waiting Roman cohort. Most of his men had little or no fighting experience. But they were enhanced now with hundreds of Roman horses as well as quality swords, shields and knives from the victory in Jerusalem. Many of his soldiers were also protected by the armor they'd taken from the dead.

It wasn't long before the Romans charged out from the village and the two sides engaged several hundred cubits outside of Eilabun. Swords clanked and dust rose amid the screams and splattering blood in the huge melee.

Simon reared his horse about in circles, hacking away at the Romans with a fearless blood-lust. Meanwhile, the Romans cut down dozens of Simon's untried troops. But the rebels far outnumbered the enemy, and they relentlessly swarmed and overwhelmed them. When it was clear that the rebels would win, Simon spotted a band of Romans charging off into the desert, fleeing the fight. He considered pursuing them, but that could lead to a trap. Besides, Eilabun was now freed from the foreign occupiers.

Once the last remaining Romans were dead on the battlefield, he ordered soldiers to rush to the village and bring back carts for the wounded and dead rebels. Meanwhile, Simon's field medics attended to the wounded with what limited supplies they carried.

Simon rode into Eilabun and was greeted by joyous cheers from the residents. Simon trotted his horse into the midst of the villagers and greeted them. His victorious rebels followed. "Our resistance army is growing. But we need more men if we are to force Rome from Israel." He was greeted by more cheers and a group of young men came immediately forward to volunteer. Simon looked around until he noticed a field of cedar trees. He told his men to follow, and they were joined by the volunteers from the village who scrambled on foot after them.

Everyone congregated near a cedar tree and watched as Simon dismounted and pointed at a cedar tree. It was neither a sapling nor an old tree. He gripped it by the trunk and tugged with all his might. At first, nothing happened. Then, incredibly, he ripped the tree from the ground. The crowd gasped and everyone looked at each other trying to comprehend what they'd just seen. It was as if they'd just witnessed a miracle.

"Any man who can do that may join my army," Simon declared. He noticed Noah, Rubin, and Levi exchanging glances as if they thought he'd gone mad. The rabbis who had followed the rebels and joined them in the aftermath of the battle all stared stone-faced, except Akiva. He was intrigued.

Surprisingly, several villagers took up the challenge. They spread out through the field searching for their trees, and it was clear to Simon that they were searching for saplings or other young trees. But it didn't matter because none of the villagers were able to uproot their tree.

Simon's men watched in confusion and at this pointless exercise. Finally, when everyone had given up, Simon jumped back on his horse and faced the crowd. "If you can't defeat an unarmed cedar tree, then you are no match for a heavily armed Roman legion."

Mumbles of disappointment flowed through the crowd. Noah rode up to Simon, and Rabbi Elazar listened from nearby. "I don't understand, Simon. Why such a test? None before had to undergo it. And you said we need more men to join us."

"I saw a lot of our men die today in the desert. They were not qualified to battle Roman soldiers. When you have scarcity, you take what you can. When you have abundance, you can be choosy, and only take the best."

Simon realized that was something that his deceased master might've said to him. He realized that he was starting to act like Leon. It was as if the spirit of his master was flowing through him, that Leon had never left him.

"There's no time to waste here. Let's go," he told Noah.

"Simon, what about our wounded?" he responded.

"They will either recover or they won't. If they can't ride, we can't take them with us. You know that. And, Noah, you should show respect and address me as sir or My Lord."

"Yes, sir."

With that, Simon rode off and his men followed, leaving the villagers staring after them.

Chapter 8

In spite of his status as prince of Israel to some and messiah to others, Simon had taken residence in Jerusalem in a house that wasn't much different from where he'd been living in the village of Kuziva. It was small and quaint with a modest courtyard, and not far from the center of the city. It was after dark when he stepped out of the front door. Guards stood on either side of the entrance. Levi and Rubin were his guards during the day and were relieved in the evening by others. Torches and lanterns burned throughout the city, and mounted men patrolled the neighborhood, enhancing his security. Though he didn't ask for it.

Akiva told him he should move to a larger, safer house where he could be more easily protected. He responded that he didn't need more security, rather, the country did. He had everything he needed right here. Almost everything. But he still felt a hole within his chest, an emptiness and that something was missing.

"Can we get you anything, My Lord?" one of the guards asked.

"No, I'm fine." He went back inside and laid on his bed.

Sometime during the night, he heard voices outside and a knock. He wondered who had knocked on his door in the middle of the night. He reached under his bed for a knife, and in a flowing motion, rolled off and onto his feet in a crouch. He didn't bother asking his guards who it was. In his thoughts, they might have knives pressing against their backs by intruders who wanted him dead.

He quickly stepped to the door, pulled it open, and relaxed. "What are you doing here in the middle of the night?"

Levi smiled. "I thought you would want to know as soon as possible."

He frowned. "Know what?"

"Her name is Ruth. I know where she lives."

His thoughts were so focused on defending Jerusalem and driving out the Romans that he'd forgotten he'd sent Levi out to look for the young woman who had somehow captured his heart. "Great. But what took so long?"

"When I went out into the crowd that day, she was gone. Then, we conquered Eilabun and I had to start over searching for her when we returned."

"Good work."

Simon was occupied most of the following day overseeing the training of troops. He'd also spent time with Rabbi Akiva reading from the Torah at the Temple Mount altar. But his thoughts drifted back to Ruth throughout the day. Finally, after dark, he made his way to her house. He had slipped out through the back door of his house to avoid the guards who would've been compelled to follow him. He knocked at her door, and a few moments later, he heard a female voice asking who was there.

"Simon."

Now, he heard two women talking excitedly in low voices. He couldn't understand what they were saying. But a few moments later, the door opened and Ruth stood in front of him looking as beautiful as he remembered. Her jaw dropped and her eyes widened. Behind her, another young woman with large brown eyes peered over her shoulder. "Hello, Ruth. I guess I don't have to introduce myself," he said with a laugh.

"No, no, you don't. This is my friend, Mary."

"Nice to meet you."

"The same. I'll let you two talk," Mary said, withdrawing inside the house.

"Would you like to go for a walk?" Simon asked.

She looked out the door in either direction. "Ah, just you and me."

"Yes, is that all right?"

"I think so. I mean, yes, yes, it is."

They walked quietly side by side, enjoying each other's company, neither one knowing what say. A mounted patrol trotted by, and the patrol leader and Simon exchanged nods.

"Your men have great respect for you."

"We share a common goal. An Israel free from oppression."

"I understand. I agree," Ruth said solemnly.

Simon felt awkward as he asked her about herself. "Have you lived in Jerusalem your whole life?"

She nodded, and tears filled her eyes. "My family is dead. My father and two brothers resisted the Romans and were... were killed. Roman soldiers took my mother and..."

Ruth struggled to complete her thought and Simon gently touched her arm.

"You don't have to say anymore," he gently said.

"I hid and got away. I've been staying with my friend, Mary and her father. She lost her mother, too. "

"I'm glad we've driven them out. I want to keep them out," Simon said.

"I hope you will. I mean, I know you will. I finally feel free for the first time. You've liberated us."

He wanted to tell her that he felt she was liberating his heart. That he'd never met anyone like her. It was true, but he feared she might misinterpret his intentions and tell him to take her back. "I couldn't do it alone. It takes the people of Israel united in the fight."

"But everyone says that without you, there would be no rebellion and the Romans would still rule Jerusalem."

"I just did what I felt was the right thing. I couldn't wait any longer."
They silently walked on.

Rabbi Akiva had heard enough of the raucous. He pounded the table, disturbing the Torahs that covered it. The meeting had broken down and diverged from studying the holy book into arguments about political strategies and tactics and personal affronts.

"Quiet! Quiet! All of you!"

The room went silent. At least as Israel's chief rabbi, he still possessed some measure of ability to control a meeting. But there was more than one rabbi who would like him replaced soon. "Now, please. We don't all need to talk at once. Tell me your concerns one at a time. Who wants to go first? Rabbi Palmer?"

"Many of us are appalled at what transpired at the village of Eilabun," Palmer said.

Heads nodded in agreement. "It was an arrogant display of barbaric strength and resulted in the loss of an opportunity to increase our numbers."

"That's true," Rabbi Elazar said. "We lost seventy-two soldiers in the attack, and many more who were wounded and will never fight again."

Mumbles of agreement met his comment.

"We grant that Simon has a brilliant military and political mind, but he barely acknowledges our traditions," Palmer said. "He ignored Passover."

Akiva was having none of it. He waved them off. "He is the messiah, which places him above our laws."

The comment sparked a burst of anger among the rabbis. "That's outrageous… not true…not true… he's a warrior, not a messiah!"

"How do you know he is the Messiah?" Palmer shouted over the others.

Israel needs a man like Simon." Several of the rabbis grumbled loudly.

Akiva looked to the rabbis who had remained quiet. Several stepped alongside him. He pleaded with his eyes for Elazar to join them, but Simon's uncle didn't move.

The discontented rabbis congregated and quietly talked among themselves. Elazar remained standing alone, watching and listening.

Finally, Akiva called out to him. "Elazar, you are Simon's uncle. What can you tell us about him, about his upbringing? We know very little."

"Yes, he is my nephew," Rabbi Elazar said. "His parents died in a fire when he was ten years old. We offered him a place in our house, but he insisted on living with a mysterious older man who was already training him to fight with a sword and a spear."

Akiva sensed that Elazar wasn't telling him the complete story and maybe someday, Simon would tell him about his upbringing and relationship with Elazar. "Who was this old man?"

"His name was Leon. I believe he was a Greek. At least, he spent many years in the Hellenic world, studying the way of the Spartans before he came to our village. Simon called him his master."

"Why did he come to your village?" Akiva pressed him.

"I don't know, but he told one of the men that the only reason he was in Kuziva was to train Simon. But that didn't make any sense to me."

"Maybe he was doing God's will."

"But that training was all about fighting and killing, not about God." Elazar raised his voice. "I don't believe he is a messiah. Not for one instant."

Akiva was taken aback by these revelations. He had never thought of Simon as someone who had a master. He'd simply thought that Simon had been born with his astonishing talents. "What happened to the master? Is he still in your village?"

"No, Simon killed him in combat. Supposedly, an accident, though I've had my doubts about that. He had told others that he had completed his training. In other words, he no longer needed his master."

"Thank you, Elazar. I will talk to him about that and ask him about Master Leon when the time is right. I want everyone to know that I continue to believe that Simon is the messiah."

The rabbis who stood apart from Akiva and his allies turned to him. Palmer stepped forward. "If we are to believe, we demand a test to prove Simon is the messiah."

"Would you ask the same of God, that he prove to you that he exists? Would you make the Almighty pass a test?" Akiva smiled. "I'm sure that God will reveal that Simon is the Son of Star in his own way, in his own time.

Hadrian scanned the lush rolling hills surrounding his villa in Tibur as his horse-drawn carriage pulled away. He was headed to the heart of Rome but he would prefer spending his day in this tranquil countryside among the wineries and magnificent gardens. Instead, he would soon sit on his ivory stool in the Curia Julia addressing the senators, and wondering which of them was plotting against him.

He arrived nearly an hour later, stopping a short distance from the senate building. Immediately, a team of eight Praetorian guards marched up to the carriage and accompanied Hadrian across the plaza and up the steps to the entrance.

He found his generals and senators in an unusually somber mood as he stepped up on the emperor's platform and sat down on his curule seat. As it was his tradition when visiting the senate, he wore his royal purple toga. He gestured toward the generals and Severus, Marcellus and Nepos approached the platform. Severus opened the proceedings: "If you and your children are well, all is well. For I and the army are in good health."

Hadrian passively nodded. "We are. Thank you, General Severus. What do my generals have for me?"

Nepos steps forward. "Though we still hold several Israeli villages…" He hesitated, nervously clearing his throat. "…Jerusalem has fallen."

Hadrian stared at him stone-faced.

"Simon ben Kosevah is behind it," Nepos continued. "His name is now Simon bar Kochva, meaning Son of Star – the Judean messiah."

Hadrian sighed in disgust. "A Judean messiah? Again?" It occurred to him that if he had not cancelled his travel plans to Britain, he might not have heard any of this for weeks and these incompetent generals might've lost control of the entire Judean province.

Nepos cleared his throat. "There's more." He motioned to a Praetorian guard who lugged a bag of coins forward and plops it before the emperor. "These are our coins re-minted."

Hadrian curiously regarded his generals, then dipped a hand into the bag and scooped a handful of what he thought were his silver denarius coins with his image on the front and Felicitas, the god of luck and good fortune on the back. But he saw something else altogether. Then he looked closely at one of the coins. "What is this?"

"It's your coin. But the Judeans struck over your image with one of the Holy Temple that we destroyed decades ago. And also, the Ark of the Covenant. On the back is an image of a Lulav – a closed frond of a date palm, which has some religious meaning to the Judeans."

Hadrian picked out one coin, turned it over, and saw that his image had been stamped over. "What does this Hebrew writing say?" he snapped, seething now.

"It says *Simon Prince of Israel* on the front and *For the Freedom of Jerusalem* on the back.

Hadrian's face turned red with uncontrollable rage, and he tossed the coins across the room. The silver metal clattered across the marble floor; coins rolled across the room. "Destroy all these coins! Melt them down! And General Severus, collect every one of these coins and send them back here."

"Yes, Your Majesty," Severus said. "It will take some time because they have spread from the capital. But we will recover them."

But Hadrian wasn't done. "This makes us look weak to our other provinces. How can you have allowed this to happen, General Nepos?"

Nepos lowered his head, expecting the worse from the emperor. He had no good answer. "They have been animated into rebellion by their new leader."

"Their so-called messiah, who has dared to put his name on our coins." Hadrian sputtered. "I order you to lead three legions into Judea, the fifth, the tenth, and the twelfth – the same ones that broke the Judean resistance in the time of Vespasian when Titus commanded the legions and destroyed Jerusalem. Send the fifth and twelfth to Jerusalem to crush the rebellion and the tenth to other cities or villages controlled by the rebels. And bring me the head of Simon, Son of Star."

Simon called a military meeting of his close advisors and officers at Mount Temple. He'd also invited Rabbi Akiva and several other rabbis. Soldiers were posted around the mount. Simon recently had begun to suspect that spies had infiltrated the growing military and that some could've been among them on missions to strike the leadership.

Weeks had passed since the rebels drove the Romans out of Eilabun, and surely by now, Hadrian had heard about the fall of Jerusalem to the rebels. Simon spent most of his time training and organizing his troops, preparing them for the inevitable attack that would come. Every day, more and more recruits from cities and villages across Israel were arriving. Some days, only a dozen arrived. Other days, it was more than a hundred. The army was growing by the thousands.

Simon also trained his officers to follow his method of preparing new soldiers for battle. He wanted strong, committed soldiers who could be quickly readied for battle. But he knew that realistically, he had to deal with the quality of those already among his troops.

"Noah, what is the current strength of our military?" Simon began.

"Close to twelve thousand."

"Good. I want you to take charge of half of them and go to Hebron and drive out the Romans. We want to secure Judea, and Hebron will be our base."

Noah frowned. "Are you certain about that, sir? Reduced numbers in Jerusalem will leave us exposed, sir."

"By now, Rome has realized that we've taken the capital back and they are planning a new incursion. My guess is that they'll flood troops into Judea because of its size. They'll want to try to break our will. But Rome doesn't know our strength. They won't know until our troops meet them head-on, first in Hebron, then here in Jerusalem."

Akiva nodded in agreement. But the others looked concerned. Noah still seemed unconvinced. "What if they come directly for Jerusalem?

Simon was undeterred. "If we need you, we will light a fire atop the Mount of Olives." He turned and pointed at it. "Instruct all villages from here to Hebron to do the same upon seeing our fire. That will be the signal to return to Jerusalem. And for all able-bodied men in the villages to join them."

"Even though the 'able-bodied' haven't passed your test?" Rabbi Palmer asked.

Simon didn't let the caustic barb annoy him. "Our need dictates our requirements." He spoke in an assertive, self-assured tone, expecting the others to abide. But he could see that all but Akiva lacked confidence in his tactics.

"We should listen to Simon," Akiva said. "He was sent by God, and God will protect us."

When no one responded, Simon said, "I would like to speak to Rabbi Akiva, Noah and Rubin. Everyone else is dismissed."

The others quickly dispersed, though some glanced back, probably wondering what other plans Simon had in mind. Then Simon turned to the remaining three when they were out of hearing range.

"I am riding to Ein Gedi to convince the people there to join our cause."

"Ein Gedi?" Akiva responded. "They're in the middle of the desert. They don't care to disrupt their lives for Israel's concerns."

"I'll try to persuade them."

"You should have a platoon to accompany you," Noah said.

"No. I'm going alone. Noah, you are to follow your orders and take half the army to Hebron and drive out the Romans. There will only be a few hundred there. It's best to take Hebron now because Rome will surely be sending reinforcements now that they know they've lost Jerusalem."

Simon turned to Rubin. "You are in charge of the army here until my return. Rabbi Akiva, see to the army's spiritual needs. You're dismissed. But Akiva, please stay."

Simon waited until Noah and Rubin were gone. "I know there's something you've wanted to talk to me about for some time and I've been putting you off because I have much on my mind. But please tell me what it is. I hope it's not about my companionship with Ruth."

"Oh, of course not. That's not it at all. You should enjoy the friendship and love of a woman, and I trust you will get married and have children before long. I see no reasonwhy the messiah cannot have a personal life with a mate."

"That's good to hear."

Akiva smiled and nodded, then turned serious again. "But that is not what I wanted to discuss with you. I think you know that some of the rabbis are doubtful about your status as messiah. I think they want to believe, but they want proof. Is there something you can do that doesn't involve just your physical strength to convince them?"

"I would think the fact that we are standing here in Jerusalem, in control of the holy city would be proof enough."

Akiva nodded. "That is a miracle and quite convincing for me. But they see you as a military leader, not the messiah."

"I don't think you want to see me float up to heaven as your proof. At least not yet. But they should be impressed by how I have turned a band of fifty rebels into an army of thousands, with more and more arriving daily. Tell the rabbis that I will turn 12,000 soldiers into an army of 120,000 and more."

"That will be impressive."

"And I will do it."

Akiva nodded. "There is one other thing. Some time ago, Rabbi Elazar told me about the man who trained you in the Spartan disciplines." He paused, and when Simon didn't respond, he continued. "Can you tell me about him?"

"Of course. He was my master. He trained and guided me in the Spartan way of combat with sword and spear. He is responsible for guiding my life as well as preparing me for deadly combat."

"Interesting. How did he guide your life, Simon?"

"He saw inside me and told me I would take a leadership role in the fight to drive out the Romans from Israel."

"He sounds like a very wise man, as well as physically adept."

"He knew every move I would make in a fight. He exerted very little effort and easily overcame my attacks on him for many years."

"What happened to him?"

Simon smiled. "I knew that was where this questioning was leading. My Uncle Elazar is fond of telling people in my village that I killed Master Leon because he was no longer useful to me. That is far from the truth."

"Tell me what the truth is, please."

Simon's face crumpled as sadness fell over him. "He told me he wouldn't live much longer. I pleaded with him not to die that I needed him, and that I wasn't ready to go out in the world yet. But a few days later, my spear pierced his chest killing him instantly. He wasn't wearing any protective armor that he usually wore under his shirt. I believe that's the way he wanted to go. Usually, he would block that thrust with a kick or step aside and push me to the ground after I missed. On that day, he let my spear connect."

Simon shook his head. "I wept and couldn't stop. Over and over, I asked him why, why did he have to die and why did I have to kill him. I wanted him to live forever."

"Thank you, Simon. We all die at some point. Some of us do while we're young, while others like me are blessed with long lives, though such lives are often fraught with trials and disappointments. For me, I want to live long enough to see Israel free of Roman oppression. Then, I will be ready to move on."

Chapter 9

Simon rode across the desert alone on his mission to attract new recruits to his army. In spite of the heat of the day, he enjoyed the opportunity again to be alone, unattended by advisors and guards. Yet, he couldn't help but imagine riding with Ruth across the desert, a romantic getaway. But that would be too dangerous. The last thing he wanted was to put that beautiful woman in any peril. Because of who he was, there would always be danger in his life, and the closer the two of them became, the more danger she would face.

As the sun was setting, he came upon intermittent small oases of trees and shrubbery, and he knew he was getting closer to the town. He rode on with the intensity of a man on a mission. As darkness fell, he stopped for the night. He would ride into Ein Gedi in the morning and request a meeting with town leaders.

He slept in the desert under the moonlight next to his campfire that kept him warm as the temperature dropped. His horse idled nearby, hitched to a lone tree. Sometime during the night, he was awakened to a rustling sound in the underbrush where he had gathered his firewood, followed by an uneasy whinny. He snatched up his sword and crept away from his dying fire, ready to defend himself and his horse from an animal attack. He froze as he heard a twig break, then departing footsteps. He waited silently, but whatever it was – animal or human – had moved on. He slept restlessly the rest of the night, his sword at his side.

In the morning, he rode through palm trees and spotted a huge oasis in the distance and the promise of a bustling village. But before he trotted into Ein Gedi, he halted his horse at the sound of crunching footsteps against loose rocks. He glanced around and suddenly, a dozen hooded men, brandishing swords emerged from behind the palm trees.

Without hesitation, Simon seamlessly slid off his horse, sword in hand. A man, nearly the size of Simon, stepped forward and threw back his hood. He was youthful, probably just out of his teens. From the scowl on his face and the scar on his broad forehead, it didn't look like he was about to welcome Simon. "Who are you?"

"I am Simon, Son of Star. I'm headed to Ein Gedi."

"We are from Ein Gedi. What is your business?" The others circled about Simon. As he talked, he remained acutely aware of their movements. It was as if he could feel their presence more than he could see them.

"I seek assistance in our rebellion against the Romans."

The man pulled his hood back up, shadowing his features. "Our leaders are aware of your conflict. They have no interest in helping."

"Many brave men have died for their freedom! For our freedom!"

"We know."

"I want to talk to your leaders."

"We will not let you pass. And there are many of us between here and the village."

Simon considered what he'd heard. It seemed the village leaders had expected a recruiter to show up at the village and ask for men to join the rebels. Before the attack on Jerusalem, Simon had sent rebels to Ein Gedi and other villages to acquire supplies and obtain new recruits. He remembered that the village leaders were happy to take rebel money for goods but were reticent about sending their young men to join the fight. But Simon thought that personal contact between him and the villagers would rectify the situation. Now, that wasn't looking too likely. "Will you pass a message on to your leaders for me?"

The hooded man hesitated, then shrugged. "What is your message?"

"Listen closely. Tell them this: 'In comfort, you sit, eat, and drink from the property of the House of Israel. And you care nothing for your brothers. Maybe God will show mercy on you. But I won't.'"

The man seemed stunned by the implied threat. With that, Simon mounted his horse, turned back, and rode away. "Don't come back, or you die!" the man shouted after him.

Simon's simmering anger slowly drained away, replaced by disappointment. He didn't like returning to Jerusalem empty-handed with no promises of help. Not a single recruit. Ein Gedi had produced no miracle, no interest in his army. Akiva had been right about that village in the desert.

He'd been riding for several hours when he came to a small oasis and spotted a deer foraging for food. He dismounted, taking out his bow and arrow that was strapped to the side pack on the horse. He moved among the palm trees, closer and closer. The breeze was coming from the direction of the deer, so it wouldn't easily pick up his scent. He hid behind a tree when he dared not move any closer. He drew back the bowstring until it creaked. The deer froze, looked around, and Simon released the arrow, striking it before it could run off.

That evening, Simon cooked strips of deer meat in the crackling flames of his campfire. The deer carcass lay nearby. After eating as much as he could, he sat by the fire in the dark. A subtle sound caught his attention. He lifted his gaze, and the firelight glistened off the eyes of an enormous, aged lion. It stood on the other side of the campfire. With just one long leap, it could take him down. He slowly drew his sword and rested it his lap.

The lion glanced at it, then returned its attention to Simon. He notices a long deep scar on the lion's left cheek. The telltale sign of a sword. He smiled respectfully, slowly stood and moved to the deer carcass. He cut off some meat and tossed it to the old boy. The lion eagerly snatched it up. He gave Simon one last look, then turned and disappeared into the night desert. Simon sighed and returned to his campfire.

The three Roman legions camped in the desert north of Jerusalem while preparations were being made for the siege to retake the capital city. Clavius climbed out of his tent shortly after daybreak, stretched his arms and gazed out over thousands of white tents. He had taken a tent on the outskirts so that he could avoid late-night rowdiness from the soldiers. General Nepos - unlike General Severus – tolerated wine-drinking and wrestling matches with soldiers betting on the contestants. The clamor was enough to awaken the desert spirits, Clavius thought. But Nepos, who was known among troops for his own consumption of wine, wanted the soldiers in a good mood and ready to conquer Simon and his rebels when the time was right.

Clavius heard the clip-clop of a horse with iron shoes and turned to see a cloaked man with scarves hiding his face ride up to the camp. He started to reach for his sword when two mounted soldiers charged over and blocked the man's path. He spread his arms to show he was unarmed and called out. "I bring you a message for General Nepos."

Clavius stepped forward and told the guards that he would take the message to the general. "Where is it? Give it to me."

"I said I would only bring a spoken message. If I were caught with a written one, I would be immediately executed."

"Fine. What is it? I'm a centurion. I'll take it to the general." The man nodded but waited until the guards moved away before telling Clavius the brief but significant message.

An hour later, he and several other centurions stood in front of Nepos who sat on a raised cushion chair in his large tent. He nodded toward Clavius. "Where's the message?"

"It was spoken only. Nothing in writing."

"Well, go ahead. What is it?"

"He said the rebel troops could number as many as our own."

Nepos considered the new information. "I wasn't expecting to hear that."

Besides his habit of excessive wine-tasting, as he called it, Nepos was also known to occasionally spread the concept of Rome's representative democracy to the military. At least, he often liked to hear the opinion of his troops before he made major decisions.

"So, Clavius, you are the only Roman soldier to have personally battled Simon and lived to talk about it. Though it was his decision to allow you to live, so you could deliver a message to the emperor. That said, what would you do now if you were the general in charge of battling Simon?"

The other centurions looked at Clavius curiously, and he noticed Felix, the cohort leader, smirking and then hissed. "Delivery boy." If Nepos had heard the comment, he sure wouldn't react. Clavius didn't care for how Nepos had laid out his failure to defeat Simon to his peers, but he appreciated the chance to respond to his request for his opinion. "I think we should surround the city and subject them to an assault by our archers. Then, move in with our infantry."

"Anyone else?" Nepos asked, obviously enjoying the moment. "Clavius doesn't know what he's talking about," Felix said and sneered at him. "Even with the size of our army, surrounding the entire city will spread us thin." With that, all the centurions started talking at once, bickering over strategies.

Nepos stood up and the centurions abruptly stopped talking. "The answer is that we only need to cut off the head of the dragon and it will die. The emperor is only interested in Simon, Son of Star. His so-called army of rebels, though surprisingly numerous, is primarily composed of farmers and common townspeople. Killing Simon will break their will."

Clavius and the others nodded in agreement. But he knew from personal experience that accomplishing that feat would not be easy."

Nepos continued, "We will assault Jerusalem from the north. This will allow some of the rebels to flee to the south. As their numbers thin, we will overwhelm them."

"But what if Simon flees?" Felix asked.

A stupid question, Clavius thought. He knew Simon wouldn't run from his army.

Nepos shook his head and grinned. "Simon won't flee. He believes himself to be their messiah, and messiahs don't run from trouble. That belief will lead him right to us. Or us to him."

A guard stepped into the tent and bowed. "Forgive the intrusion, My Lord. You

have a message." Nepos motioned him over and the guard handed him a parchment sealed with wax. He broke the seal and silently read the note. He smiled broadly and faced his eager centurions. "Another one of our spies embedded in Simon's camp says Simon has cut the strength of his army by half to protect both Jerusalem and Hebron."

"That's great news," Clavius said.

"We break camp at sunrise and move swiftly onto Jerusalem. We will seize the city and take Simon's head."

Simon rode along the city's outskirts where soldiers were posted at various points to watch for any signs of an approaching enemy force. He stopped when he reached Rubin, who was in charge of troop assignments, and asked for the latest report.

"Noah and the army attacked Hebron as planned, My Lord. They overcame the enemy easily and took control of the city. The Romans were surprised and outnumbered."

Simon nodded. By the neutral tone of Rubin's voice, he could tell that his general was still uneasy about sending Noah and half the army to Hebron. But Simon remained confident that it was the right move. "How about your scouts? Have they reported any enemy troop activity?"

"All is quiet, My Lord."

"What about people leaving?"

"Everyone is stopped and questioned. We search for anyone who seems suspicious. Just as you requested."

"Good." With that, Simon headed back into the city. In spite of the impending threat of an attack by the Romans, he was becoming increasingly concerned about enemies within, spies that were providing information on troop size and activity to the Romans.

Later that evening, he was in the courtyard of his house, sorting through a pile of armor that had been taken from the defeated and deceased Romans. He pulled out a shield that, like most, were made of strips of wood glued together to make a curve and painted red. But this one featured an illustration of an eagle that flew right above the *boss*, the iron bulge on the front that protected the hand holding the shield. He was admiring it when he heard a rustling sound and footsteps. He glanced over his shoulder and smiled.

"Hello, Ruth. Thanks for coming to see me."

"Am I disturbing you, My Lord?"

"No. And please call me Simon." He'd only seen her twice since they met several weeks ago and only for short daytime walks that had attracted the attention and gossip of residents. That annoyed him and he'd stopped seeing her. But earlier that day, he'd asked Levi to invite Ruth to come to his house that evening and informed the guards to allow her to enter.

She stared at him in a way that he found disturbing. He wondered if she was about to break off their relationship. "Why did you ask me here? I haven't heard from you for three weeks, and suddenly, your man came to the house and ordered me to come here."

"Oh, I didn't mean it as an order. I'll talk to Levi about that. You are free to leave whenever you like and I'll have a guard accompany you home."

"Well, I just got here." She looked around the courtyard that was barren, other than for the pile of armor and a circular stone grinder that he used for sharpening his weapons. "You should plant some flowers and put a table and chairs out here."

He laughed. "Maybe you could help me."

She gave him that same assessing look again and he could tell something else was on her mind. "What is it? What do you want to say to me?"

"There is something," she said shyly, then rapidly spoke, "Are you really the Messiah?"

He met her gaze. "What do you think?"

"I don't know."

He just smiled without answering.

"Are you going to build a wall around the city like you said?" she asked, switching the subject.

"That is the plan. But walls take years to build, and the Romans won't wait that long. Our primary task is to be ready to defend Jerusalem."

"Oh, really? Then, why did you send half the troops to Hebron?"

He laughed. "I didn't realize that my tactical decisions were reaching the civilian population. Who told you?"

"No one. Mary and I were out when the troops were leaving and overheard some talk in the market about what was going on."

Simon nodded and thought again about how easy it would be for a spy to find out about troop movement and report back the Roman command. "I want Hebron secured and from there; the troops can patrol the Judea countryside."

"Can we beat the Romans?"

"We?' It's not your battle."

She sternly faced him. "It's everyone's battle. We've all lost family and friends under the cruel Roman rule. We will feel the effects of that for the remainder of our lives. And if they win, who knows what will happen to those who survive."

He smiled, pleased at her firebrand nature. "If all feel as you, then victory will be assured." Now, it was her turn to smile, and he then continued. "I'm glad to have you by my side, Ruth, in this fight for our freedom."

She moved close to him and they gazed with desire into each other's eyes.

The long spears clashed at head level, Simon blocking the thrust from Master Leon, who spun about and jammed the back of his spear toward Leon's stomach. At the last moment, Simon knocked it away and thrust the side of the spear at Leon's head. But Leon ducked and came forward with the tip of his spear, driving it up under Simon's jaw. As always, he stopped short before breaking the skin.

"Your dead," Leon said. "How does it feel?"

"Same as always. Dead. I don't like it."

"Then, don't let it happen. But always be aware that the day will come. In any battle, just tell yourself it's a good day to die, then you have nothing to fear. It's a good day to die. Say it, Simon."

He hesitated, then said it, but without enthusiasm.

Leon laughed. "You're doing well with the sword. Just remember everything I told you. That's the weapon that you will use to conquer your enemies. But you need to work with the long spear. It's your backup."

"I know. Sometimes it feels awkward, especially in close." They were in Leon's courtyard as usual for the training session. But something was different about it today. The flowering bushes along the wall seemed to vibrate, their colors more intense, with a glowing halo around them. But he had no time to look any closer.

"Speed, agility, flow, anticipation. Know what the opponent or opponents will do and counter swiftly. Practice, practice, practice…and you don't even have to think; you just know. Leon laughed. "You know all this already. You're training is complete."

"Don't say that. I don't feel ready."

"Then, let's engage again. With that, their spears clashed and Simon used all his strength to force the elderly Spartan-trained warrior back. But Leon held firm, then shouted. "Someone's coming up behind you!"

Simon jammed the heel of the spear back at the imaginary attacker. Then as Leon swung at his head, Simon ducked low and swept the lower part of the spear at Leon's ankles with the intent of knocking him down, then thrusting the spear at his chest. But Leon agilely danced over the spear, then clubbed his spear at Simon's head again. Swiftly, Simon lifted his spear, blocking Leon's downward swing, then spun about and executed a backward thrust with the spearhead directly at Leon's chest. The tip struck and penetrated. Leon fell back and Simon pulled the spear away.

Leon lay on the floor and didn't move. Now it was all coming back to him. This had already happened. No, that can't be. Then to his surprise and relief, Leon leaped on his feet and scooped up his spear. "Good one, Simon. Ready to go again?"

Simon stepped back and shook his head. "No, Master Leon. I can't. You're not wearing your vest. I might kill you."

"Don't worry, Simon. You can't kill me. I'm already dead."

Simon jolted awake and sat up in bed, perspiration dripping over his eyelids. He wiped his brow. *"What a dream,"* he muttered. *"What a dream."* It had seemed so real. He'd re-lived how he'd accidentally killed his master. But now, he realized something he'd overlooked. Leon always wore a protective vest, just as he did, under his shirt. But on that day, Master Leon didn't, and he'd done it intentionally.

He heard movement next to him in bed. "Simon, are you all right? Did you have a bad dream?"

"Shh. Go back to sleep, Ruth. I'm fine."

Chapter 10

THE MASSIVE ROMAN ARMY APPROACHED Jerusalem at a leisurely pace. Too leisurely to Clavius' thinking. The rebels had controlled the capital for more than a year and that could not continue. But facing no resistance, Simon had gotten overconfident and sent half his troops to Hebron. In doing so, he'd foolishly weakened his home base. He probably thought that he could recall his troops when the Romans attacked Jerusalem and struck them from two directions. But he was wrong about it because a spy had informed the Romans about the split army, and now the tenth legion was approaching Hebron. They would overwhelm the rebels and cut them off from returning to the capital.

Meanwhile, the fifth and the twelfth were making a slow approach to the capital, as if victory were inevitable. Maybe it was, but then, Nepos had never encountered Simon, Clavius thought. Of course, Simon was only one man. But he was an inspired one and it seemed he could inspire others. How else were nine hundred Roman troops slaughtered in his rampage of Jerusalem? It seemed that none of them had escaped. If the rebels hadn't attacked Eilabun, Hadrian might still not know that Jerusalem had fallen.

This rebellion had gone on now for nearly two years and it was time to end it. Without realizing it, Clavius trotted right to the front where Nepos and his advisors were leading the way. He slowed to a walk to avoid getting any closer, but not before Nepos had noticed him. To Clavius' surprise, Nepos steered his horse over to him.

"Clavius, I'm reinstating you as a cohort leader. You're replacing Felix. I didn't appreciate his insubordination when he denigrated you out of turn in front of me and the other centurions."

So, Nepos had heard the 'delivery boy' comment after all, Clavius thought. But he couldn't take even a moment's pleasure in the shift of assignments because he knew that Nepos wanted something from him. He didn't have to wait long to find out what it was.

"Get everyone to stop right now, spread the word quickly. Set up a temporary camp. We won't be here long. Then, tell the other cohorts to meet me after dinner at my tent. And when you see Centurion Felix, tell him he's been replaced as a cohort and to attend to his own centuria. If he has any questions about that, he can talk to me."

"Yes, sir. That will be a pleasure," he thought.

Clavius rode off shouting instructions for the troops to stop. No easy task. But within a few minutes, the slow charge toward Jerusalem came to a halt. Clavius felt a new sense of power. In spite of his shortcomings, Nepos saw something in him that he liked. Maybe it was because the general knew he would be grateful and he could count on him following orders.

They only ate one meal a day, and as always, Clavius was looking forward to it. He was glad they were stopping early while still out of sight of Jerusalem. There would be no battle tonight. Felix must've gotten the message because he didn't see him at dinner when the centurions and cohorts usually ate together. He didn't trust him and would watch for the centurion who was probably sneaking around, acting like a weasel.

After dinner, the cohorts walked together to Nepos' tent. A couple of them congratulated Clavius for his return and complained that they didn't like how Felix acted on his own, always looking out for himself rather than his troops. He appreciated that he wasn't the only one who was aware of Felix's behavior. When he'd seen Felix fleeing alone from the battle at Eilabun, he and two other centurions had chased after him, intent on getting him back to the battle. But by the time they caught up to him, it was too late. The battle was lost. Clavius never reported what happened because Felix would certainly claim that he wasn't the only centurion who had fled.

The first thing that Clavius noticed when they entered Nepos' tent was that the general was not drinking wine, as he usually did after his dinner and often into the night. He stood up as they entered, and his expression was serious. "This will be brief. We will break camp at midnight, ride until dawn and set up camp outside of Jerusalem and prepare for the battle. Spread the word. Dismissed."

∽

Simon was asleep with Ruth in his arms when pounding at his door brought them wide awake. He sat up, swung his legs over the side of the bed, and pulled on a robe. He opened his door to a gray dawn and Levi who looked out of breath.

"Forgive me, My Lord, but the Romans are coming."

Simon's eyes widened but with expectation, not fear. He turned to Ruth. "Go home, stay inside. I'll send someone to take you to a safe place."

"I want to help, Simon. What can I do?"

"No! Please do as I say, Ruth. I want you protected."

With that, he quickly got ready, donned his armor, sword and shield, and rode to the Temple Mount, the highest point in the city. He joined Levi and Rubin, as well as the rabbis and a large gathering of rebel troops. In the distance, a massive Roman army was setting up camp.

"They are organizing their archers and infantry," Levi said.

"Is this their only front?" Simon asked.

"Yes, here to the north," Rubin answered.

"They will rain arrows into the city to soften us." Simon had no doubt that was their plan. "Then, they'll storm the city with their cavalry and infantry."

"Too bad we didn't build a wall in time," Rabbi Elazar commented.

"Walls aren't built overnight, Uncle," Simon answered. "Besides, if it's not complete, it's useless."

"It doesn't make sense that they are all gathered at the north side," Rabbi Akiva said. "We could escape through the south gate."

"That's what they want," Simon responded. "They are only here to take back the city."

"What should we do?" Akiva asked.

"We're going to give them a battle," Simon said. "It's just not the one they expect." He offered a sly grin as they all looked at him, wondering what he had in mind. Before anyone could ask, Simon turned to Rubin. "Get the troop onto their horses and down to the north gate."

Clavius thought that two legions of soldiers should be enough to easily overpower Simon and his amateur army, especially since Simon had sent half his army out of the city. The problem with an army this size was coordinating and mobilizing it. Getting ready for the attack was taking most of the morning. But Nepos was a veteran of numerous battles and seemed unaffected by what Clavius saw as chaos. On the front line, archers mixed with his six hundred calvary soldiers while other soldiers dug a long trench, filled it with wood and lit it on fire.

Nepos came over to him. "Get the calvary in front of the ditch and archers behind. What is wrong with them?" Some of the archers were on the same side as the calvary and some riders were still on the inside of the trench with the archers. Nepos shook his head. "Then get horses for both of us. I want you to stay close to me."

"Yes, sir." He walked between the two lines cajoling the archers and mounted soldiers that were out of place. He reached the end of the line, and then he headed over to the horse coral. Nepos' horse, a majestic prancing beast, would be all ready for him. He would have to pick out of the others that were ready to be turned out.

Just as he was about to reach the corals, he saw someone coming directly towards him from his right. He turned to see Felix. "You're very easy to pick out, you know that, Clavius? You're a big guy, maybe the biggest in the Fifth Legion. That's why Nepos likes you. You're even bigger than Simon. But you know what, you're also a big target!"

"If that's all you've got to say, get back with your soldiers. You're still a centurion, Felix."

With that, Clavius moved into the coral and secured Nepos' horse and one for himself.

He walked the horses back to Nepos. "We are almost ready, My Lord."

"Very good," Nepos said, a satisfied look on his face. Simon, Son of Star, will learn his mistake in taking on the Roman Empire. Just before he loses his head!"

Clavius grinned. But his grin quickly faded as one of the Nepos' aides rushed up shouting and pointing toward the city. "General, look!"

Clavius and Nepos turned to see the northern gate, which was elevated above the valley slowly opening, and Simon's troops on horseback surging out of the gate, hundreds, then thousands of them gathering for the attack on the Roman position. As soon as they cleared the gate, ground troops filled the city entrance and there were soldiers as far as they could see in the distance.

Rabbi Akiva stood off to the side of the gate watching Simon and the rebels ride toward the Romans. But the 'army' that filled the gate was just an illusion. Just a couple of dozen soldiers, who stood shoulder-to-shoulder, a few rows deep. It was a tactic similar to Simon's 'navy'

that had attacked Nachum. Akiva hoped that it also worked to fool the Romans about the strength of the rebel army.

"Close the gate!" Akiva shouted after the line of soldiers had moved forward.

The gate slid shut.

"It's not the entire army," Clavius shouted. "Maybe their army is bigger than we thought."

"Irrelevant for now!" Nepos snapped. "Here they come! Engage them!"

"But we're not quite prepared." The two lines were mixed up again with archers blocking the way for the calvary and some of the calvary soldiers interfering the archers' positions.

"No time!" Nepos yelled.

Clavius moved between the lines, trying to understand what happened to the order when he spotted Felix moving archers to the front side of the burning ditch where they blocked the cavalry. But Nepos was right. There was no time to confront Felix.

"Stop the rebels! Attack! Attack!" Clavius shouted.

With that, the poorly placed Roman soldiers on horseback launched forward, pushing through the archers and evading the fiery ditch. They charged ahead, galloping madly toward the oncoming rebels.

"Archers! Now!" Clavius hollered along the line.

The archers who were now on both sides of the ditch, dipped their oil-soaked arrow tips into the flames. Then, they raised the arrows skyward, drew back their bowstring, and launched their flaming arrows. In spite of the chaos on the lines, the arrows soared skyward filling the sky.

The thunderous charge of thousands of galloping horses spread across the valley as Simon and his army rode hard toward the Roman camp.

Overhead, flaming arrows blotted the sunlight. The rebels raised their shields without slowing. The arrows thumped against the shields, many sinking into the wood. But some found rebel bodies, and they tumbled from their horses. Simon's army continued their advance, undaunted.

The two armies collided with a terrifying clash of steel. The battle ensued close enough to Jerusalem, so that residents could hear the clanging of sword against sword, shouts and scream of men and horses as chaos reigned on the battlefield. Blood spurted. Bodies fell. Horses trampled on the fallen, breaking bones and crushing heads. It went on and on.

Nepos and Clavius remained in the rear with the archers as they watched the battle from atop their steads. "Get our archers on horses with swords. We need to overwhelm the rebels."

"My Lord, I've tried that before," Clavius began. "I'm not sure how…"

"We've got no choice. Get every available man out there! Including yourself!

"Yes, sir."

He was about to hurry away when Nepos reached over and grabbed his forearm. "Which one is Simon? Can you see him out there?"

Clavius scanned the crowded field of combatants and spotted him on foot, slashing away at Roman soldiers who were all around him. He pointed. "There! That's him. The big guy!'"

"No bigger than you. Get out there. Kill him!

Clavius nodded. Sword in hand, he rode toward the throng of fighters. He lost sight of Simon, then spotted him again, several horse-lengths away. But Clavius was no fool. He ordered another soldier, a burly young Roman recruit, to join him and pointed out Simon.

"That's him? That's Simon?" the soldier said.

"Let's get him!"

The soldier cut in front of Clavius and charged forward toward Simon. As soon as he was within a horse length of Simon, he raised his sword and was immediately pulled from his horse from behind by another rider. He landed at Simon's feet and was instantly slain by the rebel leader. Clavius noticed that Simon had his own team of fighters with him on foot and on horseback, each one hacking down Roman soldiers as fast as they came at them.

He considered retreating but knew that Nepos was probably watching him. He was about to charge forward when rebels came at Clavius from either side, blocking his path to Simon. They were smaller and less experienced fighters, and Clavius took them on one after another. But more kept coming and he couldn't get any closer to his target.

Along with Levi and Rubin, Simon stood his ground and battled one Roman after another. The bodies were piling up, getting trampled and the screams of the fallen continued until their death. Next to him, Rubin fought two Romans, slashing with his sword and then lost his footing on the bloody terrain and fell onto his back.

The Romans raised their swords to finish him off, but Simon responded in a flash, slashing one across the throat and piercing the other in the gut, both collapsing. He extended his hand to Rubin, pulling him to his feet. "I can't lose my most valued general."

Rubin nodded and they momentarily made eye contact. Then, they quickly returned to the battle. Since he was on foot, Simon couldn't tell how the battle was going. Yet, he sensed it was turning in favor of the rebels. He'd no sooner come to that conclusion when he heard shouts from the Romans calling the calvary to withdraw.

Chapter 11

Ruth opened the door and cautiously stepped out into the cool night air. The streets were dark and eerily quiet, as if the city had been abandoned. No torchlight illuminated her way as she moved away from the house. Everyone was staying inside, fearing an attack from the Romans. The rebels, it seemed, had held them off today, but she knew the Romans weren't about to give up so easily. They had controlled Jerusalem for the past sixty years and they wanted it back. If the rebellion collapsed, the retribution would be brutal. Anyone who had served as a rebel or aided them would be subject to torture and condemned to death.

In spite of the city's overwhelming joy in the aftermath of the rebel victory, an unease had prevailed among the civilian population. Residents had quietly talked about the inevitable assault the capital would face when the Roman legions returned. After all, they had not only lost the capital city but nine hundred of their soldiers.

She was disappointed this morning when Simon told her to go home, that there was nothing she could do except hide. She hated living in fear and wanted to help in any way she could. She'd returned to the house and told Mary and her father that the Romans were outside the city preparing to attack. Her father, who assisted the rebellion by coordinating supplies for the troops, had immediately left to see how he could help. He told them to stay inside and someone would come to lead them to one of the underground tunnels that had been created centuries ago.

Ruth, though, was determined not to hide. If she went into a tunnel, she wouldn't be allowed to leave until the threat was over, and that could be days, if not longer. She'd no sooner told Mary she would stay behind when a rabbi arrived at the house and said he was there at the direct order of Simon to take Ruth and any other women to a tunnel. Mary glanced over at Ruth who shook her head. "It's just me," Mary told the rabbi. "I'll go with you."

"Then, let's go, Ruth, no time to waste," the rabbi said, mistaking Mary for Ruth, and they left.

Ruth had waited inside all day. She'd heard the distant fighting, then the quiet. Night fell and there were no soldiers on the street. No one at all. She walked quickly through the darkness toward the north gate. To her surprise, the gate was open and illuminated by firelight from outside the city. She cautiously moved forward until she saw huge bonfires along the perimeter where hundreds of rebel soldiers were camped.

She ambled through the gate and moved through the camp. She gasped as she moved past rows of bloodied bodies laid out for families to claim. Nearby, she heard moans from a large tent and knew that the injured were being treated by the rebel medics. After a few minutes, she spotted Simon talking with Levi, Rubin and Rabbi Akiva. Simon stopped in mid-sentence when he glimpsed her approach.

"It's not safe here, Ruth. You should stay in the tunnels."

"I didn't go there. I stayed in the house. Why are you outside the gate?"

"A show of strength. We're holding off the Romans."

"But for how long?"

Simon scowled, getting annoyed with her for questioning him in front of the others. "For as long as necessary."

"I'll stay with you," she said defiantly.

"No!"

"Yes!" Ruth replied.

He seemed surprised at her sudden assertiveness. Levi and Rabbi Akiva looked away, embarrassed at Ruth rejecting Simon's order.

Simon looked past Ruth and called over Levi.

"Yes, My Lord."

"Please escort Ruth back to her house. Post two... no... four guards there."

Levi nodded. Ruth glared at Simon, annoyed by the way he was ordering her to leave, but she turned away without another word and went with Levi.

Rubin cleared his throat. "As I was saying, our men reached the Mount of Olives hours ago. The message has been sent."

Simon glanced to the mountaintop where a huge fire burned. "Let's go see if it's working."

"I'll stay here and you can tell me what you see," Rabbi Akiva said with a laugh.

Simon and Rubin followed the path to the top of Temple Mount, the highest point in the city, but lower than the nearby Mount of Olives. A rebel team of four had broken off from the army, climbed to the top of the mountain, and started a massive fire to signal the rebels in Judea. Simon and Rubin stopped at the same place where they'd stood early that morning after the Roman legions had been spotted at daybreak. A lot had happened in one day. Simon's armor had saved his life during the battle more than once, and his chest and back was aching with bruises. But he was thankful that he was alive. He also knew that it wasn't over. The Romans had retreated, but they hadn't given up.

He looked down the mountain at the array of torches where the Romans were camped and planning their next move. Then, peering out toward the southern horizon, Simon was elated to see fires burning on several mountaintops in the direction of Hebron. As they gazed out, another distant fire started.

"It's working," Rubin said. "The message has been sent. But it'll take days for our troops to make it back from Hebron."

Simon nodded. He knew they needed to hold off the Romans in any way they could until the reinforcements arrived. He came alert as he heard footsteps that sounded like several people moving their way. One of the rebel scouts appeared out of the darkness, followed by several rebel soldiers. He gasped for air, trying to catch his breath.

"My Lord. We were able to get close to the Roman camp. A third legion has arrived."

Simon considered what he'd just heard. "Thank you for that," he said and dismissed the soldiers. He turned to Rubin. "I need you now to go to Jericho tonight to deliver a message. Get a fresh horse, meet me at my house, and be ready to ride through the night."

Even though Rubin was battered and one of his arms was bandaged after being sliced by a Roman sword, he was tough and committed to the rebel cause. Simon had made him a general and put him in charge of the new recruits showing up to join the rebels. While his close friend, Levi, was tall and thin, Rubin was stout and strong. He wasn't short, but he appeared to be to some because he was so broad in the chest and shoulders.

When he arrived at Simon's place, he waited while Simon finished preparing the scroll. "Here it is. Take it to the large church in the square. Wake up the priest. We need their support right away."

"I'll go as fast as I can." With that, Rubin mounted his horse and headed for the notorious trail between Jerusalem and Jericho, known as the "Way of Blood." It obtained that name because of the blood that was often shed in attacks along the trail by robbers.

It was midnight when Rubin arrived at a large stone structure. He dismounted and pounded on the massive door with its metal knocker. After a couple of minutes, he heard a key turning in a lock on the door. It creaked open and a priest stared suspiciously out.

Rubin held up the scroll. "I have an important message to the people of Jericho from Simon, Son of Star, the leader of the rebellion. It can't wait until morning."

In less than an hour, the priest had gathered three church elders and read from the scroll.

It is time that all residents of Israel come together to drive the Roman occupiers out of our country. We request your assistance in our fight against the pagan Roman worshippers. Please join us in this conflict which serves our mutual interests.

Signed,

Simon, Son of Star – our Messiah.

The priest raised an eyebrow at Rubin, who anxiously fidgeted. "... Simon, Son of Star... our Messiah. The priest shook his head and the church elders mumbled in disgust at the word 'messiah.'

The priest rolled up the scroll and handed it back to Rubin. "We have but one messiah, and it is our Lord, Jesus Christ. We will not replace our messiah and our able men will not join your ranks.

Rubin hung his head in despair, then turned away.

Sunrise. The fires outside the north gate had burned out, leaving charcoal, wisps of smoke, and the lingering smell of campfire. The army was awake, the soldiers milling about, looking from time to time toward the Roman position as they prepared for another day of battle. Simon was meeting with his generals as they considered what would be the best strategy. The rabbis had just joined them and offered their encouragement when Rubin rode up.

He was exhausted and nearly tumbled off his horse. He approached Simon, frowned and shook his head. "They refused to help us."

Simon bristled with anger. "So be it." They all stared out toward the Roman camp and saw the cavalry, infantry, and archers forming lines within an arrow shot away.

"I still think we should wait for Noah and our reinforcements," Levi said.

Simon shook his head. "Doubtful that we'll have the luxury."

"But shouldn't we stay inside the city and wait?" Rabbi Akiva wondered.

"Without any resistance, they'll invade and swarm the city," Simon responded. "They will be in our midst and upon us. Best to hit them head-on."

"They're on the move!" Levi said. The Roman lines began to advance on the city.

Simon swiftly mounted his horse and shouted. "Move out!

All down the rebel lines, captains repeated the order. Rabbi Akiva stepped up and faced the other rabbis. "Let us pray to God for protection."

Simon, suddenly energized and ready for the fight, guffawed at the rabbis. Then looking skyward, he called out, "Oh, Master of the Universe, there is no need for you to assist us against our enemies, but do not embarrass us, either!"

With that, Simon yelped a battle cry and galloped toward the Romans, followed by thousands of troops, all shouting out their own battle cries.

The rabbis were left in the dust puzzling over Simon's odd comment. Rabbi Palmer glared at Akiva. "Was that our messiah test? If so, how did he do?" he asked, sarcastically.

"You might be more of a believer once he saves our lives," Akiva snapped. Then, turning to the others. "Everyone inside! Close the gate!"

A storm of arrows bombarded the rebels. Again, most were stopped by shields, but some soldiers were mortally wounded. The calvary and infantry on both sides clashed, swords clanged, horses whinnied, and fallen soldiers cried out in agony.

Simon, Rubin, and Levi remained relatively close to each other. They dismounted and engaged the Romans again on foot. Simon hacked away and cut down Romans as fast as they came near him. As the battle continued, the rebels held their own in spite of being outnumbered.

The rabbis watched the battle with trepidation from Temple Mount. Rabbi Elazar pointed toward the far side of the battle. "Oh, no. Look what's coming! This is very bad."

They all shifted their gaze and saw tens of thousands of new Roman troops gathering at least three legions. One legion broke off and rode south, giving the battlefield a wide berth. "They're heading to the rear of the city," Palmer said. "It's undefended. No one will stop them from entering the city."

A second legion stormed the battlefield. Now the rebels were dangerously outnumbered. Akiva fell silent and stone-faced. Finally, the third new legion charged in behind the second one. The rebels were not only far outnumbered but were overwhelmed.

"We need to go," Palmer said.

Akiva sadly nodded, and they all climbed down Temple Mount to their waiting horses.

Thousands of fresh Roman soldiers swarmed the field and hacked down rebel soldiers. Blood flowed as bodies carpeted the valley floor. Simon, Noah, Rubin, and Levi formed a circle facing outward, barely holding their own against the onslaught. How long could they carry on? Simon wondered. No matter how many Romans they killed, there were more to replace them. Simon conceded the fight today was lost.

He knew one thing for certain. He would never surrender. He would fight to the death, but he wasn't ready to die today. That left one option. They could retreat and re-group with the rest of the army.

"Withdraw! Withdraw! Rendezvous in Hebron!"

Rebels spread the word to withdraw.

Simon and his fighting team battled their way to their horses, slashing and cutting down Roman soldiers. He mounted his horse. Levi did the same. "I'll see you in Hebron," Simon shouted, then looked back and saw Rubin lying face down next his horse. He wasn't about to leave him behind.

He dropped to the ground and was immediately attacked by two Roman infantry soldiers. He clashed swords with one, pushing him back, then slashed his sword at the other one who, to Simon's surprise, blocked it with a long spear. He spun about and took down the first soldier with a slicing blow across his throat. He immediately moved in close to the spear-bearing soldier so that he couldn't use his weapon. The Roman reacted by pulling out a knife and thrusting it at him. But Simon was ready for him and buried the end of his sword under the soldier's rib cage.

He turned, stuffed away his sword, and picked up Rubin, a feat in itself, and somehow had the strength to toss him onto the back of his horse. He was about to mount the stead when three Romans on horseback surrounded him. "That's Simon!" one of them shouted. "Take him down!"

A blood-covered sword sliced through the air at his head but Simon ducked, then dove forward and snatched the spear from the fatally wounded soldier. He leaped to his feet and jammed the long weapon into the gut of the soldier. He toppled over and his horse ran off, dragging the Roman by one foot.

Another soldier charged at him, swinging his sword. Simon blocked the blow, then slammed the spear against the side of his head, and the stunned soldier retreated from the fight.

"Behind you!" a voice yelled and Simon thrust the foot of the spear into the soldier's chest and he fell to the ground. The Roman started to get up but before Simon could react, Rubin slashed his throat with his knife.

"What! I thought you were dead!" Simon shouted.

"No, I just passed out, too tired. I woke up when you threw me on the horse."

Simon shook his head in disbelief. "Let's get out of here."

They rode toward the city as fast as their horses would take them, and Simon yelled to other rebels. "Withdraw! Withdraw!" As they raced toward the city, hoofs pounding the turf, Simon glanced back to see they were being chased by the Roman calvary.

General Nepos gloated at the arrival of the two additional legions on the battlefield. The surging Romans were quickly overpowering the rebels. "Goodbye, Simon. It is over. You have lost."

Clavius stood stoically beside him, passively watching the massive melee. Bodies littered the battlefield, more rebels than Romans. It was just a matter of time now, he thought. The rebel army was decimated. Soon the Romans would be inside Jerusalem again and taking control. If Simon wasn't among the dead, they would hunt him down, along with the rest of the remaining rebels hiding in the city.

"They're retreating! Nepos said. "It's over. Get the horses. We're going into Jerusalem and finishing them off."

"Yes, sir."

Chapter 12

Rubin rode into the north gate with Simon at his side. He felt terrible that he had collapsed on the battlefield and endangered Simon, who had refused to leave him behind. He wanted to show Simon now that he was ready to fight. Hundreds of rebel troops were gathering near the gate, uncertain what to do. Rubin expected Simon to call on the troops to fight the Romans to keep them out of the city as long as possible. But to Rubin's surprise, Simon called for the troops to abandon the gate and fight the Romans on the streets.

It didn't take long for Rubin to see why he'd made that decision. Roman troops were already in the city. "They came in through the south gate," Simon shouted. "Follow me."

Rebel troops engaged the Romans on the streets, blades striking bodies, blood flowing, and bodies tumbling. But Simon avoided the main streets and galloped down the narrow passageways and Rubin couldn't help thinking that he was avoiding the Romans. That was not the Simon he knew.

Finally, after several twists and turns, Rubin realized where Simon was taking him. He should've known. They stopped outside Ruth's house, where three guards were stationed. The guards came to attention at the sight of Simon who leapt off his horse. Rubin did the same, then stepped back as Ruth opened the door and flung herself into Simon's arms.

"You're alive. I was so worried. What's going on? Why are there Romans in the streets? There was fighting right out here! One of the guards was killed."

That's when Rubin noticed several bodies of Roman soldiers piled near bushes in the space between the two adjoining houses. Separate from them was the fallen rebel soldier.

"It's not safe anymore in Jerusalem. You need to go," Simon said.

"I want to stay with you."

"No!"

Simon turned to him, and Rubin knew what he was going to ask. "You and the guards take Ruth to Hebron. I'll meet up with you there."

Rubin couldn't help thinking that Simon felt he could no longer rely on Rubin as a fighter. "I guess you don't trust me to fight by your side after what happened on the battlefield."

Simon frowned at him. "Not true. I trust you to take care of Ruth. Get on your horse right now. You've got to go."

Rubin followed the order, then Simon assisted Ruth onto Rubin's horse as the guards mounted their steads. Simon firmly grips Rubin's arm. "I am entrusting you with her life. You know the secret way out of the city."

"Is it safe?"

"Safer than trying to get out of the city any other way."

Rubin nodded. "I will serve you well, My Lord." He just hoped he didn't fall asleep and tumble off his horse. He hadn't slept for two days.

Simon slapped the rump of Rubin's horse. "Go! Go!"

One of the guards accompanying Rubin on their quest to escape the city had lived his entire life in Jerusalem. Samuel, who was just eighteen, knew all the back streets where there was less chance to come upon Roman soldiers. But it was taking much longer than Rubin liked. They had been only a few blocks from the entrance to the secret escape, but going directly there would've meant a good chance they would've encountered Romans. With Ruth on his horse, he would be greatly handicapped in any combat.

Finally, they had one street to cross to reach their destination. Samuel stopped near the end of the alleyway and turned to Rubin. "There are soldiers nearby. They'll see us. I'm going to charge out there and distract them. That's when you cross and walk your horses through the narrow passage."

"Samuel, that's too dangerous," Ruth said. "They might catch you."

He smiled at her. "I'm fast and know places to hide. I can get away. Besides, I don't want to go that way with you. It's too frightening for me."

"Why is it frightening?" Ruth asked.

"You'll find out. Get ready. I'm going." With that, Samuel rode out of the alley and turned down the street.

"Hey, there's one!" a soldier shouted. "Get him!" Several horses thundered away and Rubin and the two remaining guard crossed the street, dismounted and quickly walked their horses down a passage that was so narrow the horses were scraping along the walls. Finally, the passage expanded as they arrived at an arched door that was wide enough for the horses. Rubin pushed on it to no effect. He tried again, this time, pushing with his shoulder, and it came slightly open. The two guards gave a shove and it opened all the way. They entered a tunnel with torches burning every few paces.

As soon they were all inside with horses in tow, Ruth gasped. "Oh, no! Look! I heard about this place. Now I know why Samuel wouldn't come here. They say it's haunted."

The walls were stacked with skulls, one on top of another. Thousands of them. Their hollow eye holes stared out toward anyone passing by. The horses stomped their hoofs and whinnied. "I knew there were some skulls," Rubin admitted, leading the way. "But I had no idea. Let's get through to the end."

They moved ahead, careful to keep the horses from hitting the skulls. Torch lights flicking off the skulls seemed to animate them and left Rubin feeling uneasy, as if he and the others were being watched. He tried to look straight ahead and wondered how much farther they had to go.

The tunnel looked as if it was about to come to an end when Rubin saw that it turned down another passageway. Now, the skulls were accompanied by thigh bones crossed below each skull and the passage seemed to shrink around them. Fewer torches lit the way and they moved forward at a slower pace. Finally, they came to a door. But when Rubin pushed on it, he couldn't budge it. He struggled with it and the two guards joined him. They pushed severally to no effect.

"Wait," Ruth said. "Maybe you're going the wrong way." Rubin paused, pulled on the wooden handle, and it slowly opened. "Thanks for the help, Ruth," he said with a laugh.

Daylight flooded in as they made their way out of the tunnel and out of the city.

Nepos, with Clavius close behind, charged into Jerusalem and immediately found themselves in the midst of fighting. The general hadn't expected the strength of the resistance and was surprised at how many Romans were lying in their blood on the streets. But he was certain that it would be just a matter of time before their soldiers put down the last of the rebels. The fighting turned furious as they moved farther into the city. A rebel was surrounded by Romans, but he was cutting them down, one after another.

"That's Simon!" Clavius shouted.

Nepos dismounted and motioned Clavius to stay close behind him, then pulled out his sword and strode toward Simon. "Simon bar Kochva! Son of Star!"

Simon spun about at the sound of Roman calling him by name. He spotted Clavius on his horseback and smiled. "Yes, of course, the one I let live has spread the word."

He met Nepos' gaze. "From your purple garments, I see I'll be adding a general – royalty, in fact – to my list of kills today."

"I am General Nepos. And this will be the last face you gaze upon."

They both moved purposefully toward one another and their swords clanged off the other's shield. They slashed and parried. Nepos held his own against Simon, who was probably exhausted from a long day of killing Romans. They continued parrying, clanging, and slashing without damage. On and on.

Thinking Simon was weakening, Nepos charged at him. Simon quickly backpedaled, stumbled and fell, and his sword slipped out of his hand, tumbling out of easy reach. Simon quickly glanced around. A crowd of Roman soldiers has formed to watch. The street was littered with rebel bodies.

Nepos moved in for the kill and slammed his sword downward at Simon's head. But Simon quickly raised his shield and blocked the blow. Nepos pulled back his sword again, holding it high overhead with both hands ready to slash open Simon's throat before cutting off his head. But in that moment, he'd left himself exposed and Simon swiftly slid his arm out of his shield and hurled it like a disc striking Nepos' face. He trundled backwards, barely maintaining his footing, then recovered and charged forward again.

Simon scrambled for his sword, snatched it, jumped up, and spun around just in time to block Nepos' blade, steel slamming against steel. Simon pushed the general back, stepped forward and sliced his blade across Nepos' chest, scoring a superficial wound. In rapid succession, he slashed twice more across Nepo's chest. The general's confidence started to wane with the wounds as he realized that Simon's abilities to survive and attack seemed beyond normal. A moment later, Simon knocked

Nepos' sword out of his and held his sword to the general's throat. Their gazes locked and the crowd grew silent.

"I let your centurion live to deliver a message. Now it's time to deliver another one. With that, he ran his sword through General Nepos' chest and killed him. The moment after Nepos crumpled to the ground, Roman soldiers swarmed forward, piling on top of Simon.

Chapter 13

Torches burned throughout the city of Hebron as Rubin and Ruth arrived, flanked by the two soldiers who had accompanied them. They had barely entered the city when they were met by more rebel soldiers on horseback, who gave them skins of water. They drank like they hadn't had a drop of water in days, then one of the rebels told them to follow him. They were escorted farther into the city, and after a few minutes arrived at a large building.

A roaring fireplace warmed an expansive, high-ceilinged room where Rubin and Ruth were greeted by Levi, Rabbis Akiva, Elazar, and Palmer. Ruth anxiously scanned the soldiers in the room with hope in her eyes. "Where is Simon?"

Everyone exchanged concerned glances. "We thought he was with you and

Rubin," Levi said, focusing on Rubin; his facial features were taut. "What about the troops in the city after the withdrawal?"

Rubin solemnly shook his head. "It didn't look good. We barely escaped the city. Hope faded from everyone's eyes. Levi bristled with a desire for action.

"Simon told us to rendezvous here so we could regroup with Noah's troops but they're not here. These soldiers are all from Jerusalem."

"Where is Noah? Where are his troops?" Rubin asked.

"They left Hebron for Jerusalem the day before, but they never made it," Levi said, leaving unsaid any speculation of their fate. "I'm heading back."

"What do you mean?" Rubin asked.

"I'll take a small band of soldiers. If Simon is alive, we'll find him and get him out."

"I'll go with you," Rubin said.

Rabbi Palmer shook his head. "This is foolhardy. Why go back there? Surely Simon is dead by now."

Rabbi Akiva glared at him. "I realize you doubt he is our messiah, but I do not. We need him. Our people need him."

"We'll do whatever it takes to rescue him," Levi vowed.

Palmer looked exasperated. "There are thousands of Roman troops in Jerusalem. That's suicide."

Levi was about to respond when Ruth spoke up. "Not if it's done right."

The men turned silent and eyed Ruth with surprise.

"The way Simon would do it."

Levi looked at her curiously. "Explain."

Ruth met his gaze. "I will."

Simon woke up on a floor of a room covered in dirt; the room was dark and smelled of urine and feces. His entire body ached from the severe beating he'd taken at the hands of his captors. Yet, he was still alive. He lifted his head and felt a sharp pain. He couldn't sit up, couldn't move, and quickly realized he was bound in heavy chains.

The last thing he remembered was Clavius hovering over him as he laid on the street bleeding. "A quick death is too good for you. But you are going to wish you were dead! The gods will tear you apart. You will die many times over waiting for your real death."

Clavius kicked him in the gut. "Speak, Simon, Son of Star. What do you say now?"

"I will cut off the head of your leadership."

With that, Clavius kicked him in the forehead and everything went black.

He was still wandering in his subconscious mind, trying to figure out how he got there and how long he'd laid there. Suddenly, the door creaked open and bright sunlight struck him like shards of glass piercing his eyes. He squinted and saw a large shadowy figure fill the doorway. "Time to march through Jerusalem, Messiah," Clavius said and laughed. Soldiers moved in, pulled him to his feet, and dragged him outside.

"Stand up and walk!" Clavius ordered.

The soldiers released him and Simon collapsed to the street. Clavius rolled him over and grabbed him by the throat. "You walk, or we drag you down the street."

Availing all the energy he could muster, Simon pulled himself to his feet and took a couple of tentative steps in the chains. "Take off the chains and I'll walk better."

Clavius laughed. "I don't think so. I like you walking in chains or I could drag you behind a horse. Your choice."

Simon took a few short hesitant steps, pausing after each one. Simon, a cluster of Roman soldiers and Clavius led the way as they moved slowly down the street. Every sluggish step was painful, but Simon refused to fall down and be dragged to wherever they were taking him. But after a dozen steps, he tripped over the chains and dropped to his hands and knees.

"Pull him to his feet and hold him up," Clavius snapped. "Now walk, Son of Star."

His head hung as they continued down the street. He could hear voices of the Romans on the street jeering him and more disturbing sounds in the distance of people in distress. They turned to a corner and now he heard cries of anguish and screams much louder.

Clavius grabbed his jaw and lifted his head. "Look! Look, Simon!"

He blinked, clearing his vision, and he couldn't believe what he saw. A dozen or more of his rebel soldiers were crucified in a courtyard. They were still alive, hanging, moaning, and weeping in pain. Others screamed as they were held down and nailed to crosses.

"Your rebellion is over, Simon, Son of Star. After your death, we will hunt down the rest of your rebel scoundrels and put each one of them to the sword."

Simon stared at him defiantly. Clavius smiled in response.

Hadrian and Sabrina, emperor and empress, followed the long walkway from their villa, past flower gardens and shrubbery, finally emerging to the stables where Hadrian's carriage awaited him. He was dressed in his imperial robe, purple with fine gold threading and she wore a long white gown. Several slaves stopped what they were doing and bowed their heads toward the imperial couple.

"Carry on," Hadrian called out. He was proud of how well he treated his slaves and he'd made a law that slave owners could no longer kill the people they owned. He turned to Sabrina. "Are you sure, my love, that you don't want to go to the palace today? We have something to celebrate with the capture of the rebellion leader in Judea."

"Why is he still alive? He should've been beheaded immediately and his head hung in the center of Jerusalem for all to see."

Hadrian laughed, though he thought she might be right. "Maybe you should come and lecture the general about it."

She shook her head. "No, thank you. I prefer to spend the day with my young nieces and my nephew. I want to enjoy them while they are young. Especially since it seems we will never have any of our own."

From the deprecating tone of her voice, it was clear that she felt their lack of children was his fault. But he already knew that. She might be right, too, he thought, since the few other women he had laid with never became pregnant either. But when she talked like that to him, it just made him think of Antinous, the true love of his life.

"Then do enjoy the privileged little monsters," he said and smiled as he climbed into the carriage and the driver pulled away.

An hour later, Hadrian's carriage moved through the streets of Rome and his palace came into view. Two weeks had passed since he'd been here. Although he preferred the villa in Tibur, he admired the sight of the morning sunshine glistening off the impressive palace and how the magnificent city stretched beyond it as far as the eye could see. He was met by Praetorian guards and Generals Severus and Marcellus, who waited outside the palace for his arrival.

Hadrian nodded curtly to them and they entered the palace in procession and moved briskly along the marble hallway, the general on each side of him. "The news has left me with mixed feelings," he said to the generals as they walked. "It's wonderful that we've caught this Simon, the leader of the rebellion. But it saddens me that we've lost General Nepos."

"Don't dwell on it, Your Highness. He will always be remembered and honored for leading the campaign that captured the rebel leader and bringing the rebellion to an end."

Hadrian suddenly stopped and his entourage did the same. He brought a finger to his lips as he considered the general's comment. "But has the rebellion ended?"

"Without their leader, Your Highness, I would think…"

"This Simon has planted a seed of an idea, and ideas are much harder to kill than people." He paused, mulling over the matter. "We need to make an example of him. Let me think." He paused again, nodded to himself. "Yes, I want this so-called messiah taken to the amphitheater in Caesarea. Invite his people to see how well he fares against a lion."

Hadrian turned crisply and faced Severus. "General Severus, since you are already the commanding general of Judea, I want you to see to it personally. Deliver him to the amphitheater and make sure that the lion is very hungry."

Severus gave him a quick bow of the head. "Yes, Your Highness. Is there anything else I can do for you?"

Hadrian waved a hand. "Dismissed."

With that, Severus swiftly went on his way.

Ruth, Rubin and Levi slipped into Jerusalem the same way she and Rubin had left the city. This time, she did her best to ignore the profusion of skulls. But Levi was acting as if he were frightened out of his mind and urged them to go back out and find a different way into the city.

"This is the safest and quickest way, Levi," Rubin said, and Ruth added: "Don't look at the skulls. Just follow me and Rubin."

"I believe they protected us on our way from here to Hebron," Rubin said in an assuring tone.

Grudgingly, Levi agreed and followed.

They quickly passed through, found the street empty, and crossed into the heart of the city. They headed to the house where Ruth had lived with her friend, Mary, and her father. Ruth wore a cape with the hood up because out of the three, she was the most easily identifiable as someone associated with Simon. Yet, she had insisted on contacting Mary and her father as their first choice for finding out what happened to Simon.

"Don't worry, you two. I'll be fast. And maybe I can find out something. Just watch for soldiers. But don't engage them."

"I wouldn't think of it," Rubin said. "Unless they went after you."

"We'll stay out of trouble," Levi assured her. "But hurry."

Ruth tapped on the door, then tried the handle and it opened. She cautiously stepped inside. "Mary, are you here?"

Her friend emerged from the bedroom she shared with Ruth. Surprise and astonishment rippled across her features. "Quick. Close the door." Mary hurriedly closed the door, looked up at Ruth, and with total joy and excitement, they hugged each other tightly. "I've missed you so much, Ruth. But what are you doing here? It's dangerous for you."

"I know. Has there been trouble for you?"

"No, not so far. But I've stayed off the street as much as possible. How are you?"

"I'm fine. What have you heard about Simon? Is he alive?"

She shook her head. "I'm sorry, Ruth. I don't know. I haven't dared to ask because the Romans are looking for any excuse to capture or kill anyone they suspect to be working for the rebels."

The door burst open and Ruth spun around to see Mary's father walk in. He saw her and stopped. "Ruth, you shouldn't be here."

"I'm sorry, Ben. I'm just here for a moment. I wanted to make sure you and Mary are well. I'm also trying to find out what happened to Simon. Have you heard any--?"

"He's not here."

"What do you mean by that?"

"He's alive or he was. They came for him with an entire legion two days ago and took him away. "

"Where were they taking him?"

He shook his head. "I don't know. But someone said the legion was headed to Caesarea. So, maybe there."

"Thank you." She hugged him briefly, then hugged Mary again. "See you soon, I hope," she whispered to Mary." Then hurried out.

At the direction of Severus, Clavius led a Roman legion across the desert and into the coastal city of Caesarea. Seagulls cried out and swept over the soldiers as they made their way along the beach. Clavius raised his hand, halting the troops as they approached more Roman troops. A centurion holding a vine-staff approached. Clavius guessed he was leading a Roman cohort.

"Do you have the prisoner?" the centurion asked.

"Of course."

"I'm to take him to a holding cell. He is to be prepared for the amphitheater," the centurion said.

Clavius led him to a metal cage drawn by horses. Simon sat inside, his chest and arms bound in chains.

Simon gazed out through the barred windows of the cell where he'd been taken after he was removed from the cage. He'd been here two days and no one had told him why he was transported here, or where he was, though he knew from the smell of the air and the call of seagulls that he was near the sea. He heard a commotion outside and turned to see Roman soldiers marching up to him. They stepped aside for a general, who stopped in front of the rusty bars and peered in.

"Simon, Son of Star."

Simon looked him over like a superior officer judging a soldier. "That's who I am. Who are you?"

"I am General Sextus Julius Severus of the Roman army."

Simon blankly stared at him.

"You are to order your army to surrender and recognize Roman authority."

"And if I don't?"

"You will be put to death."

"And if I do?"

Severus blinked a few times, caught off guard by the question.

"I suspect I will still be put to death."

The General remained silent.

"I refuse to make your job easier, general. So get on with it. You're wasting my time."

Simon turned away, leaving the general staring at his back.

He was sure the reason that he'd been brought to this coastal city was related to some sort of torture or exhibition of his death. But why here? There must be someone or something here that required transporting him to this city. He didn't think it was Severus, but maybe it was the emperor. He was convinced that Hadrian had something to do with it.

Days went by and Simon was fed once a day and given a jug of water. He had a pot for his toilet, which was cleaned daily. A medic came and examined him. He was told they wanted him healthy to fight. He asked who he would be fighting, but the medic and guard didn't respond. He hoped it was the big Roman, the one he'd spared. This time, he would not offer him the same grace as he did before. But why take him here?

One day he found the answer when a guard mentioned that the amphitheater was ready for him. He knew immediately that an amphitheater was like a smaller version of the Roman Coliseum, where criminals, runaway slaves, and Christians were fed to the lions while Romans gathered to watch. He realized that would be his fate.

After that, he began allowing his mind to drift to the past, his private times with Ruth when they explored each other's bodies and merged. Other times, he went back to his years with Master Leon. He remembered that one day he'd asked Leon what had prompted him to become a master of Spartan martial arts. That's when he'd learned that Leon's parents had both been killed by Roman soldiers in the aftermath of the first rebellion. He was nine years old at the time and vowed that he would grow up to be able to defend himself against the Romans and he would pay them back for killing his parents.

Yet, Leon would not kill Romans just because they were Roman soldiers. Instead, he waited for confrontations instigated by the soldiers. One day, when Simon was fourteen, Master Leon showed up for a lesson after he'd been gone for several days. One of his arms was wrapped from a wound he'd received in an encounter with three soldiers outside another village. He confessed that he'd made a mistake and taken his eye off one of them for just a second and it had given the soldier an opening to attack. Yet, Leon had still managed to kill all three. But he had to go into hiding to avoid a *centuria* of soldiers that hunted him after the incident.

Simon told him that he wanted to join him on his next journey and help fight the Romans if they were confronted. Leon had shaken his head and said, "Not until you're sixteen."

Two years later, he asked again and Master Leon had agreed to take him to Jerusalem. But to Simon's surprise, Leon said they would take no weapons on their journey. Outside of the capital city, a patrol of three soldiers had stopped them, asked their business, and Leon had said they were visiting friends and buying supplies. With that, they were allowed to pass.

"Why didn't we fight them?" Simon had asked. "They were young and inexperienced. We could've easily disarmed them."

Leon shook his head. "They made no effort to threaten us. They don't want to be here. They were forced into the military."

"How do you know that?"

Leon laughed. "How do I know anything? Experience and an ability to judge men."

"Did you know their thoughts?"

"It's more about what they were feeling than what they were thinking."

But once in the city gate, they were confronted by a drunken, belligerent older soldier who was training a younger one. He told the soldier, "This is how we do it." He grabbed Leon by the throat and put his blade to Leon's eye and demanded that he give him his money.

In a startling swift move, Leon disarmed him and cut his throat. Simon simultaneously disarmed the younger soldier and felled him with a kick to his head. "Leave him be," Leon said and they slipped away into a crowd before more soldiers arrived. "You will have plenty of opportunities to kill Romans," he told Simon as they walked through the market undetected.

After that, all it took was for Leon and Simon to travel anywhere and they would eventually be stopped somewhere on the road by Romans. Sometimes they spared them, other times, they killed them.

Simon wanted to be just like Leon, a one-man army killing Roman soldiers who threatened him. But Master Leon told him that wouldn't be his destiny.

On the day of his execution by a lion, Simon was asleep on a floor pad when he was awakened by the footsteps approaching his cell. Soldiers filled the barred doorway and one of them shouted, "Prisoner, rise!"

Soldiers surrounded Simon and shackled his wrists. He was led on a horseback towards the amphitheater. Romans gathered on either side of the road and shouted at him:

"Die, you rebel trash!"

"Where is your Judean god now?"

"Maybe you should call upon Apollo to save you!"

Laughter flowed through the crowd along the street, but Simon ignored them. With little hope left, he found a thought to focus on. Lions, unlike vengeful soldiers, don't torture their kill. Most likely, Simon's neck would be quickly snapped and his throat ripped out. He would be dead in seconds of the lion striking its prey. But maybe he could somehow survive. His thoughts drifted to the story of Samson in the Holy Scriptures. Samson was able to fight a lion and managed to kill the beast. *Will God give me this strength as he did with Samson?*

Chapter 14

Pain and longing filled Ruth's eyes as Simon rode past in shackles, surrounded by Roman soldiers. She wore the same hooded cape she'd worn in Jerusalem but she wasn't too worried about being recognized here. Israelis and Romans were mixed in the crowd that followed Simon's horse towards the amphitheater. Those that were already seated, roared when two soldiers marched Simon on his horse to the center of the arena. They pulled him off and each soldier grasped one of his arms.

An announcer, standing in an elevated wooden booth near one wall, spoke in a loud voice that reached the closest repeaters in the crowd: "Our entertainment today is Simon bar Kochva…self-proclaimed Judean messiah…and leader of the Judean rebellion." His words were shouted throughout the crowd by the assigned repeater and boos filled the amphitheater.

"Now, here is our brave General Sextus Julius Severus, who captured the traitor."

Severus waved to the crowd, acknowledging the cheers as he walked out to the center of the area. He stepped in front of Simon and met his cold stare. Then, he spoke in phrases allowing the repeaters to spread his message. "Simon, Son of Star… you have been found guilty of treason by Emperor Hadrian…. Your sentence is *damnatio ad bestias* - condemnation by beast." Repeaters throughout the crowd could be heard echoing Simon's sentence.

Ruth was shaking under her cloak as the general walked away and took a seat in the front row. A soldier unshackled Simon and quickly left. The gate slid down leaving Simon alone and unarmed. He looked thinner than she remembered him and limped slightly. How were they ever going to help him escape? Her plan was worthless as long as he was trapped inside the amphitheater and facing a hungry lion. She hated the idea that she was here to see her Simon slaughtered and eaten by a horrific beast. There must be some way that she could help him get away, but how?

The announcer spoke again: "Let us now witness Simon's fate… proving that the Judean god…is a false god…who will not…and cannot save him."

A gate opened and a snarling lion entered the amphitheater. Ruth watched in horror as Simon looked around for a weapon but there was none. He backed up as the lion stalked towards him. The lion suddenly stopped about five paces in front of him. Ruth knew that with one leap, the beast could pounce on Simon and lock its jaws on his throat and strangle him.

The lion leaned forward and stared hard at him. Simon returned the stare, then gaped in disbelief. The lion had a familiar scar on its left cheek. It was the same beast Simon encountered in the Judean desert. The one he'd fed. Simon tentatively extended his arms in a submissive gesture. The lion cautiously approached and sniffed him. Simon ran his right hand through its mane, and the creature leaned into the hand, as if it were a massive dog.

"You too will be killed by the Romans when they are through with you." He spoke in a soft re-assuring voice. So let us both bid them farewell." In one swift move, Simon mounted the lion as if it were a horse. The crowd gasped in surprise. They'd never seen such an exhibition.

Simon tightly held the lion's mane. It bucked several times, not sure what to do with this man on its back. Then, Simon dug his heels into its sides as he would a horse and lion sprinted forward.

Simon guided the galloping beast to the lowest section of the amphitheater's wall and dug his heels into its side. The lion leaped over it and landed among the spectators. Terrified shouts and cries echoed throughout the amphitheater. The crowd jumped to its feet and the spectators began fleeing for their lives.

Simon hung onto the lion's mane as it trampled over screaming Romans who had come to watch the lion shred him into pieces. He steered the lion toward a ramp that he hoped led to a way out. The lion cut to the left at the sight of an arched opening and they raced out onto a street that paralleled the Caesarean amphitheater. But the soldiers ran outside quickly and surrounded Simon and the lion, who stopped dead at the sight of their swords. Simon looked around, searching for an escape route.

Suddenly, his attention was drawn to a crowd of cloaked Romans fleeing the amphitheater. A woman threw her hood back and Simon was shocked to see that it was Ruth. But before he had a chance to react, soldiers charged him with their swords raised and ready to strike. The lion mauled the nearest soldier, instantly killing him. Simon leaped from the beast, rolled and snatched up the dead soldier's sword.

The other Romans gave the lion a wide berth and let it follow its instincts and run off, disappearing down the street, as residents screamed and took flight. Simon quickly cut down two soldiers with his blade, spilling their blood on the street. But he was hopelessly outnumbered and the Romans were closing in on him from his left, right and in front of him. Behind him, a crowd of residents were blocking his escape. He held his ground, ready to fight and die. He caught a glimpse of Ruth again among the Roman residents, but she hastily slipped away.

Suddenly, he heard his name called out from behind him and it was a familiar voice. The crowd behind him threw off their cloaks revealing swords. They were rebel troops, led by Levi and Rubin.

"We are here for you, My Lord," Levi called out.

They rushed in, flanking Simon, and engaged the soldiers, who were now outnumbered. Swords clashed and clanged as they parried and slashed. Blood spilled all over the place. Roman and rebel soldiers were felled. Bodies cluttered the road as the fighting continued until Rubin rushed to Simon's side and pointed with his sword. "This way, My Lord!"

"Where's Ruth?"

"Don't worry," Rubin answered.

Simon scowled at Rubin. *He better be right.* Levi joined them and they fought their way down the side street. Rubin led them to a stable and quickly motioned them inside. It was filled with horses and Ruth was there. Simon hugged her tightly as rebel troops rushed into the stable.

He was relieved to see her but angry that she was there. He turned to Rubin. "I entrusted you! You shouldn't have brought her!" Simon's muscles flexed with rage.

Ruth grabbed his shoulder. "I made him bring me!"

"This was her plan, My Lord," Rubin said.

Simon was stunned. He smiled at Ruth and realized that she was as cunning as he was. "Maybe I should make you one of my generals."

She beamed at that.

"Let us take our leave! Quickly." Simon mounted a horse and to his surprise, Ruth mounted one of her own. He had underestimated her in more ways than one, he realized.

Dozens of horses stampeded from the stable carrying Simon and the rest. They headed for the outskirts of the city.

Severus and his entourage of soldiers, including Clavius, bolted down the ramp, the general's cape whipping behind him. Clavius had been surprised that Severus had refused to leave the amphitheater until he'd heard that the lion had been killed. Apparently, he never wanted a chance for an encounter with the beast, which might've picked up his scent.

Once they were out of the amphitheater and on the street, they surveyed the carnage of dead soldiers stretching for several blocks. "One man and a lion could not have accomplished this much killing," Severus said.

"No sir. He had allies who were hidden among the residents of the city," Clavius said.

"That is obvious, Centurion," the general snapped.

A wounded rebel soldier near him moaned in pain. "Rebel scum," Severus hissed, then viciously sliced his throat with his sword.

"General, should I dispatch a messenger to Rome to inform the Emperor of what has transpired here?" Clavius noticed Severus flinch slightly at the thought.

"This news will not bode well. I will deliver it myself to Emperor Hadrian. Ready my consortium. We'll leave in the morning."

"Yes, My Lord." Clavius moved off, stepping through the bodies.

Simon and his rebel pack rode for hours at a steady pace and were approaching the town of Gophna when he raised a hand calling for a halt. Levi and Rubin conveyed the order and the troops ambled to a stop.

"We will set up camp here." Simon turned to Rubin. "At sundown, go to the top of the mountain and light the fire just as we did when we were alerting the troops. Let all of Israel know that Simon, Son of Star, lives."

"My Lord, the fire will also alert the Romans."

Simon laughed. "So be it. They will find out soon enough anyway."

The troops began to dismount and set up camp.

That evening, Simon and Ruth sat by a campfire, quietly conversing. Rebel troops patrolled the outskirts of the campsite where Simon's remaining rebel troops, numbering in the hundreds, had assembled. He told her that while he was captive, General Severus had boasted about how the tenth legion had destroyed half his army. "My strategy failed, Ruth. Noah and the army were slaughtered. It was my fault."

"Simon, you're being too hard on yourself. You're not responsible for the loss of the troops. Noah was the general, not you. He was there, not you."

"But I made the decision to send him and the troops to Hebron. I thought it would be a powerful tactic to show how strong we were and to catch them off guard, but it didn't work. Rather, they caught us off guard instead. They never made it back to Jerusalem."

"Why didn't it work?" Ruth asked.

Simon thought a moment, then raised his head and stared at her. "That's the question, isn't it? The reason is that they knew about the troops in Hebron and that we were weakened in Jerusalem."

"How did they know?"

"They were told, that's how. There's a spy among us who gave the Romans all the information that they needed."

"Who would do that, Simon? Who would turn on their own people?"

"I wish I knew, Ruth."

She moved closer and placed an arm around his shoulder. "I'm glad I'm here with you. We will sleep together tonight…"

Simon frowned. "But you know you shouldn't be anywhere near me. It's too dangerous for you."

"The safest place for me is at your side."

He shook his head. "Not if we are attacked. As soon as possible, I want Rubin to take you to a village where you'll be safe."

Now, it was Ruth's turn to frown. "You may order your troops around, but I am not a part of your army. I am my own person and I make my own decisions."

Simon shrugged. "Actually, you are part of my army, especially since you orchestrated my rescue. Everyone with me now is in my army. All men, women, and children. That is how we will defeat the Romans."

"Then, what becomes of 'us' when that conflict is over? Can the messiah take a wife? Can he have children?"

Simon wasn't sure what to say. Just then, Levi walked up and pointed to the mountain top. "Excuse me, My Lord, Rubin has lit the fire. They all looked to the flames licking high into the sky.

A rebel soldier shouted and pointed to the south. "Look!"

They followed his gaze. A fire had already started in response on a distant mountain. Then, another one on an even more distant mountain, and another. "Our allies in the cities and villages had been prepared."

"They must have been encamped on each mountain for weeks. Just waiting." Levi said.

"Such loyalty will set a good example," Simon said, proudly.

Rabbi Akiva was having trouble sleeping. At his age, that was hardly unusual, especially in a strange bed here in Hebron, a city that he hadn't visited for many years. But this time he thought he'd heard a noise that had awakened him. He slowly sat up and realized someone had knocked at his door.

"Come."

The door opened and Akiva was startled to see Shimon bar Yochai. He wiped his face, brushing away the sleep. "Rashbi, my son, what are you doing here in Hebron and what are you doing waking me in the middle of the night?"

"Sorry, Master Akiva. I had a call to come to Hebron. But I didn't know you were here until I arrived in the city less than an hour ago. I saw Rabbi Palmer standing in the street and he told me that you were here."

Akiva scowled. He was pleased to see his best pupil, a scholar from a young age, and the only one of two of his students whom he had ever ordained. Under Hadrian's rule, it was extremely dangerous to ordain a rabbi. Both the rabbi and the student could be condemned to death. They had not seen each other in months and the sight of Rashbi brought joy to his heart. They were so close that he thought of him as a son. Yet, he was annoyed that he had been awakened from a deep sleep. "Palmer should have found you a bed and you should have greeted me in the morning."

"Of course, that is what I would have done, Master. But something important is being revealed in the sky and the rabbis are gathering on the street."

With that, Akiva stood up and pulled on his robe. Now, he was curious and concerned. "Let us go and see."

They stepped outside and indeed, rabbis and others were gathered on the street and many were looking up at something.

"Rabbi Akiva. Come see. Come see," one of them called out in an excited voice.

"What is it?"

"He lives!"

He joined them and gazed at a distant mountain where a bonfire flickered in the night. "Of course, he lives. He is the messiah."

Akiva glanced over at Palmer and Elazar who both looked disappointed at the news. He would have none of that. "Wake everyone! Tonight we celebrate. And we have Rabbi Shimon ben Yochai joining us."

"About time," snapped Palmer. Where have you been, Shimon? I know Akiva has missed you dearly. He could've used your help."

Shimon was slender and bearded with rounded shoulders from decades of scholarship, but he was no coward, as Palmer implied. He gave the rabbi a withering look. "I have supported the rebellion in my own way. I am a scholar, not a warrior. But I am here now to assist Akiva in any way I can. I fully support the rebellion. How about you?"

How inciteful, Akiva thought. He and Rashbi had been inseparable until Akiva had first seen Simon battle the Romans single-handedly in

Jerusalem. At that point, Akiva knew he would be following a new path that would take him away from Jerusalem. Shimon was ready to follow him and Simon, but after some lengthy consideration, Akiva encouraged Shimon to continue teaching the Torah to students at a secret location. Laws of the Holy Scriptures had to be kept alive in spite of the Roman directives. Shimon was disappointed but agreed.

Akiva was greatly encouraged by the news that Simon lived and with Rashbi here, it was truly a night to celebrate. But sadly, he knew the Romans were also aware and would be roused to continue their assault on Israel.

❧

From his throne, Hadrian threw up his hands in disgust and stared at Generals Severus and Marcellus. "How could this have happened? How could he have escaped? How could he still be free and alive after nearly three years? He's making a fool of me and fools of you! It weakens our grip on other provinces."

"Your Majesty, his army invaded Caesarea, hundreds, probably thousands of them. He was rescued before he could be killed." Severus spoke without meeting the emperor's gaze and Hadrian had doubts about what he'd heard.

Even if it was true that Simon's troops had flooded the city, it didn't explain a very odd part of the story that senators had whispered and that had been passed to Empress Sabina. His gaze narrowed as he peered at Severus. "Is it true that Simon, Son of Star, tamed that lion at the amphitheater?"

"It is true that the lion did not attack him," Severus said, attempting to explain what he'd seen with his own eyes. It was not fed for a week by its keepers to make it hungry for a kill. But it seems that the lack of food had the opposite effect. The lion was too weak to attack Simon, and he took advantage of that."

"And how exactly did he take advantage of that situation, general?"

"That is the extraordinary thing. He was somehow able to ride the lion like a horse and escape the amphitheater."

"Extraordinary, indeed." Hadrian paused, considering what he'd heard. "How did the Judeans of the city respond to this?"

Several skirmishes erupted between them and our soldiers. But the rebel troops had left, so they were easily put down."

"So, they were inspired by him?"

"Yes. It seems that they were."

"Then we must act immediately before we have rebellions appearing everywhere, not just in Judea. This is a serious matter." Hadrian weighed his options. He turned to Marcellus, who so far had said nothing. "General Marcellus, gather the might of the Roman legions from Britanya and Gallia to crush Simon! I want you to catch him before he and his band can expand their army again with new recruits."

"Your Majesty, our legions are thinning. Moving more could compromise the security of...."

Hadrian bristled with anger. "Just do what I commanded, general."

Marcellus bowed. "Yes, Your Majesty. It will be done." He hurried off.

On another rebel campsite, the moonlight shone on Jerusalem in the distance.

Simon and Levi were sitting by their campfire when they heard a familiar voice call out to them. They came to their feet as Rubin rushed towards them from the darkness. He dropped by the campfire, exhausted.

"My Lord, a Roman patrol was spotted close to the camp. There were three of them. Our patrol killed two of them, and we captured the third one. What should we do with him?"

Simon thought a moment. "Tie him up and put him in a tent. Let him go in the morning when we leave. He can deliver a message that we're not done. We're just getting started. We'll go to Hebron and gather the remaining troops we have left there and the rabbis. We must pick up as many allies as possible and establish a new training base in the mountains, east of the Dead Sea. Rome will not sit idle after their embarrassment in Caesarea."

Levi smiled. "I can only imagine how Emperor Hadrian responded to the story of your escape from the lion that was supposed to eat you."

"Well, it helped that I knew the lion."

Levi and Rubin exchanged looks, not sure what to think or believe.

Simon and his troops rode into Hebron and were astonished at the sight. The city had been burned to the grounds and in total ruins. Some buildings were still in flames, others had been smoldered.

He led his soldiers slowly down a street strewn with bodies of civilians. But he didn't see anyone that he recognized as rebel soldiers or any robed rabbis.

The sound of footsteps caught his attention and he spotted a man trying to hide behind a charred wall.

"You! Come here!' Simon shouted.

A wiry elderly man cautiously stepped out, his face twisted in fear. He prostrated himself in front of Simon. "Please don't hurt me, sir. I'm not any threat to you."

"Stand up. I will not harm you." Simon noticed the movement of people watching from hiding places. He raised his voice. "I won't harm any of you. Please come out."

The man meekly came to his feet. Suddenly, more men, women and children appeared from the remains of a nearby building. They called out to the others and soon, hundreds of residents of the destroyed city had gathered. "Help us!" a strapping young man shouted and stepped forward. "The Romans destroyed everything."

"What happened here? Where are my soldiers? Where are the rabbis?"

An older woman moved closer to Simon. "Your soldiers didn't stay and fight. There were too many Romans, too few of the rebels. They fled with the rabbis."

"They told us to hide," added a tough-looking man with charcoal streaks on his face. He waved a hand. "But you can't hide when they burn your house down!"

"We had no defenses after your soldiers left," another young man said. "We pleaded for our lives." He pointed at Simon. "They said they did this in retaliation because of the rebel leader. You!"

The crowd glared at Simon, blame and judgment in their eyes. Even Simon's men exchanged questioning glances.

Levi curiously looked at Simon. "The Romans got here ahead of us? Why

didn't they engage us in the desert?"

Simon felt unsettled. His confidence wavered slightly. Maybe he'd miscalculated his tactics and underestimated Rome's fortitude. "They're trying to break the will of our resistance."

"How are we going to survive?" a woman holding a baby called out.

"Give her some food and water," he told Levi, then dismounted. He climbed to the top of a one-story structure. "People of Hebron! I am so sorry for your losses. We did not get here in time to stop the Romans. You need to understand that your only chance of survival is to align yourselves with me -- Simon, Son of Star -- your messiah! We will rebuild your city when the time is right."

Gasps rippled throughout the crowd. Some seem pleased to hear this claim, some shook their heads in disbelief, and others seemed undecided, but curious. "I command every able-bodied man to join us. Your very freedom depends on it. Bring every weapon you own. Even metal tools if you don't own a weapon. We must re-establish our army as quickly as possible."

His comments were met by a combination of cheers and boos. An old villager stepped up. "Why should we follow you? We've already lost everything because of you."

Simon stared harshly at the old villager. Then his face softened. "Would you be so selfish as to see the same fate fall upon your fellow Judeans?"

The old villager backed away, his face flushed with shame.

Simon scanned the crowd. "Who is joining us?"

No one spoke or responded. Simon waited.

Finally, the first man they'd encountered, the one who had feared them, stepped forward. "I will do what I can. I'm not a fighter. But I can cook."

"Good. Who else?" Simon stared at a young man who had spoken up. He nodded and stepped forward. "I'm with you." He turned and called three names and the young men moved to the front. Then followed by several others.

"There are more still hiding. We can get them," one of the men said.

"Then go get them, gather your people, weapons, and report here as quickly as you can," Simon said. "We need to leave soon."

Less than an hour later, Simon and his troops rode away from the heavily damaged city that smelled of soot and death. They galloped into the desert in rows, the first with Simon and Ruth side by side, each succeeding one larger than the one before it so the troops formed a moving arrowhead. Their numbers were now increased in the hundreds.

Simon's plan was to lead them in a southerly direction to the oasis city of Ein Gedi and he hoped he would be welcome this time. At least he wanted to find out if that is where the troops and rabbi went after they fled Hebron. He had sent soldiers there to buy food and supplies when they were training at Mount Nebo for the attack on Jerusalem. But when he had gone there on his own to attract recruits, he had been turned away and he hadn't forgotten that.

Levi rode up alongside Simon. "We have added three hundred."

"Weapons?"

"An assortment of short swords, shovels, and hammers. About a dozen archers with bows in various states. But hundreds of arrows."

"Better than the numbers and weaponry from whence we arrived," Ruth shouted as if she were one of the soldiers.

Levi smiled and nodded. "That's true."

Simon didn't like that Ruth was riding up near the front with him. But he was committed to protecting her. So the closer they were together, the better. At least until they were attacked.

"How much longer, Simon?"

"We'll reach Ein Gedi by late afternoon."

Rubin had left Hebron before the others and ridden into the desert to scout their route. After more than an hour of hard riding, he passed through the remains of a recent encampment with still smoldering campfires. He stopped and searched the area, then spotted Roman troops milling about in the desert as if awaiting orders. They were probably the same ones who had destroyed Hebron. They hadn't noticed him yet. So, he quickly left the old encampment and rode back the other way until he intercepted Simon and the troops.

"Romans up ahead," he yelled. I don't think they know we're here."

Simon shouted for the troops to halt and the word quickly spread. "Let's avoid a confrontation now. We'll head east towards the Dead Sea and go around the Romans to get to Ein Gedi."

Simon motioned everyone to turn east. Rubin took one look back from the direction he'd come and hoped that none of the Roman soldiers had trailed him.

After riding east for nearly two hours, Ruth called out to Simon. "Can't we stop and rest for a while?"

He was about to snap that they were at war and there was no time for resting. But then he realized that not only was Ruth tiring but so were the new recruits who had never served in a military campaign. He raised a hand, slowed his pace, then called out for everyone to stop and take a break.

He helped Ruth off her horse and she thanked him. "I think everyone will appreciate at least a short rest."

Simon looked around. They were still in the desert but he knew if they kept going, they would reach cliffs and valley around the Dead Sea where they would be more camouflaged by the natural surroundings. He didn't like stopping because when he did, he started reflecting on all the soldiers that he had lost in battles and how weak his army was now. But he couldn't stop;so, it was either they continued going and somehow rebuild the army or die.

He walked around and talked to the soldiers, especially the new ones. He saw that Levi and Rubin were doing the same. Ruth stayed by his side and he could tell from the looks of the men that they wondered what a young woman was doing among them. They didn't know that she'd saved his life. He answered their questions, told them that they would be leaving shortly and riding the remaining distance to the Dead Sea where they would camp for the night. Simon noticed that his battle-tested soldiers were already getting back on their horses. He knew they didn't like being exposed on the desert and not moving.

One of them who was back on his horse shouted and pointed in the distance. A cloud of dust had appeared on the horizon. It was moving in their direction. Rubin rushed up to Simon. "What do we do, My Lord? Do we flee?"

He shook his head. "They've already seen us." He knew stopping had been a mistake but didn't say it aloud. "We hold our ground. That's all we can do."

From the size of the dust cloud he could see, it was no more than a few hundred soldiers, not a legion. He shouted orders, telling his new recruits to stay on the ground, and for his seasoned soldiers to mount their horses, which they were already doing. He told the archers to get ready but not to fire until he ordered them.

He turned to Rubin. "Take Ruth, get your horses and go. Get to the sea and wait."

"I'm not leaving you, Simon!" Ruth said. "If you die here, so will I."

"Do as I say. Now!"

"No!"

"Rubin...take her."

"Come on, Ruth." Before she protested further, Rubin scooped her up, threw her over his shoulder, and carried her back towards the horses. Simon followed, making certain that she abided. She scowled at him, then mounted her horse. Rubin did the same and they rode off.

Simon, meanwhile, leaped onto his own horse and rode over to his other mounted soldiers who had moved a couple hundred paces in front of the line of archers. A scout was racing toward them and he went out to meet him. "How many are there?"

"Hundreds. But it's our troops, My Lord. The ones from Hebron."

The soldiers upon hearing the news relaxed and some laughed. "Stay alert!" Simon ordered. Look at the dust cloud behind them. The Romans might be coming after them."

"No, sir. Not the Romans. Those are the rabbis with more soldiers."

The reunion in the desert was joyous, with everyone intermingling, soldiers who had trained together in Jerusalem and elsewhere reunited. Simon, in particular, was pleased to see the aged chief rabbi still on his feet. "So good to see you, Rabbi Akiva."

"Likewise, Simon. I never gave up hope that you were still alive and would be free again, and here you are."

"You were fortunate to get out of Hebron before the Romans arrived," Simon said. "They destroyed the city and slaughtered everyone they could find."

Akiva nodded sadly. "Some of the soldiers wanted to stay and fight, but I knew it was futile." He looked around. "It's terrible about Noah and all of his troops. Our numbers are so small now."

"Better than they were before you arrived, Akiva." With that, Simon called everyone's attention and the soldiers quieted down and turned to their leader. "We are united now and we are stronger. We will camp here for the night. Then early tomorrow morning, we will continue on to the Dead Sea.

A cheer went up. When it died down, the soldiers were dismounting their horses, and Simon helped Akiva down from his stead. Akiva smiled and looked over Simon's shoulder. "My Lord, I think there's someone here to see you."

Simon turned and there stood Ruth and Rubin. "Sorry we missed the party," Ruth said, sarcastically.

"She insisted we come back to see what happened," Rubin said. "I couldn't stop her."

Simon smiled and hugged Ruth. "I'm not surprised, Rubin."

Chapter 15

It was mid-morning when the Dead Sea came into view and Simon was feeling better about their chances of not only surviving against the Romans but establishing a stronghold. They were now fifteen hundred strong and he was sure that they would be able to gather more volunteers in the months ahead and create a larger and more qualified army. But the important thing in the present moment was to avoid the remaining legions of the Roman troops that could easily overwhelm and slaughter all of them.

They'd left the desert landscape behind and were now moving slower among cliff and valleys as they neared the sea – the great sea where nothing lived. He didn't like that thought but they'd been forced in this direction to avoid the Roman troops in the desert. When they reached the shoreline, Simon turned the troops to the south and they continued on.

The beach was wide but gradually narrowed when piles of large rocks appeared. They moved at a slower pace and the line of soldiers narrowed. Not far ahead, beyond the rocks, a steep cliff rose to their right with the sea to their left and an open space in between where the troops could gather for a break before moving on.

"You like this place?" Simon asked as they neared the cliff. Ruth considered his question for too long, he thought.

"It looks nice here, but I don't know. I don't feel good about it."

"It looks good to me." He tried to sound hopeful, but her concern seemed to infect him.

They reached the base of the cliff, stopped and waited for the troops to catch up. No sooner had more than half of the troops entered the open area when arrows rained down from the top of the cliff. Shouts and screams followed as many of the arrows hit their mark.

Simon reached over and grabbed the reins of Ruth's horse and shouted: "Against the wall!" He swiftly led her close to the cliff and others followed ducking out of the sight of the archers. Arrows continued flying, pelting and killing the injured who hadn't been able to seek safety in time.

Simon hadn't caught his breath yet when a shout went up from the rear of the line where soldiers had stopped to avoid the cliff and arrows. "The Romans are coming!"

Simon dismounted and cautiously stepped away from the wall but kept out of range of the flight of arrows. He peered down the line of soldiers and saw what they were seeing. Roman troops on horseback were charging down the side of a valley, stampeding towards them. From the sound of the hoof beats and rumble of the earth, he knew they numbered thousands.

"What are we going to do, sir?" Levi asked, coming up next to him.

He didn't know the answer. "The troops in the desert were a diversion to drive us this way. They were waiting for us."

"Should we turn and confront them?" Levi asked.

Simon shook his head. "We don't stand a chance confronting them directly. Look at what we've got, a battered army with a few hundred additional refugees against thousands!"

Simon looked at what lay ahead past the cliff if they stayed on the path. A series of very narrow paths leading into a deep rift. Simon brightened as an idea took form. He quickly mounted his stead and shouted. "Follow me! Everyone! Ride like the wind! As fast as you can!"

The message was passed along and everyone bolted for the rift valley. Arrows reined again, striking only a few rebels. They stormed into the narrow valley in a single file, clearing the range of the archers.

∽

The Roman legion, led by General Marcellus, slowed as it approached the valley entrance. Clavius was at his side as protector and guide. As always, his large size had given him benefits in spite of his shortcomings. Now, he took advantage of his position and shook his head. "General, I don't like the looks of what's ahead. It could be a trap."

Marcellus waved a hand. "We've got them far outnumbered. We will enter the valley in a single file. That's all we can do." He turned to Clavius. "Unless you want to give up on catching Simon again. You know how well that will go in Rome."

He nodded grimly, then edged his horse to the side and motioned for the next soldier to pass through. After several had entered without incident, Clavius and the general followed. The soldiers entered the valley single file but they were so heavily armed, their horses so massive, and the trail so rugged that it was cumbersome to move faster than at a slow walk.

After a couple of thousand troops had entered, Marcellus came to a stop. He realized there were too many and the passageway was clogged with horse and riders. "Clavius, go back, and take all the men who haven't entered this passage yet around to the other side of the valley. Engage the rebels as they leave."

Clavius blinked several times. "But General, it will take us over a day to go around the mountain."

Marcellus gives him a withering look. "You're wasting time then."

"Yes, My Lord."

Clavius retreated, working his way through the current of slowly moving soldier to where others were still entering the rift. He stopped the next one who was about to enter the rift and told him to back up and turn around. He shouted for everyone to turn back and told them they were taking a different route.

Simon and his soldiers reached a wider section of the valley. He stopped and raised a hand. When everyone had gathered as close as they could on their horses, he said: "Levi and I will stay here with our experienced fighters. Rubin, you lead the rest on through the valley until you're clear. Then guide everyone to Ein Gedi, the oasis, as swiftly as possible."

Simon met Ruth's longing gaze. "You go with Rubin." Her features turned sad, and he knew she didn't want to go. "We'll reunite in Ein Gedi. I promise you."

To his surprise, she didn't argue. She stepped forward and hugged him. "I'll be waiting for you. Don't disappoint me." She turned away and moved on.

He watched her go off deeper into the valley with Rubin and the refugees from Hebron. "Levi, let's split our archers equally, six on each side and have them climb as high as possible up the two faces of the cliff."

Levi nodded and went to work.

Everyone was in place, waiting near the passageway leading out of the rift. The Romans couldn't be much longer, Simon thought. The lookout had already spotted the first soldiers in the distance and reported back. But their pace was slow.

Finally, a single file of Romans came into view. The lead soldier picked up his pace, moving into a hard trot. He saw the way out and wanted to get there as quickly as possible. "An opening lies ahead!" he shouted.

That was good enough for Simon. He rose up from the elevated alcove where he was hiding. His sword flashed in the sun as he swung it and lopped off the soldier's head. His body fell limply backwards and off the horse.

The second rider's horse hurtled over the dead soldier. As he landed, Levi appeared on the other side of the opening and rammed his blade straight through the rider's heart. He tumbled off his horse, landing next to the other Roman's head.

The soldier behind their fallen Romans pulled up short and his horse reared up. The line came to a stop and that was when the archers from the cliff showered the stalled soldiers with arrows. Screams, shouts and whinnies followed as soldiers and their horses collapsed on the trail. The rift was soon clogged with bodies trapping in the narrow passage with no way to turn around. Simon's soldiers ran out from hiding and hacked away at the stalled soldiers. Forced to go forward, they urged their horses ahead and collided with those directly in front of them. Some abandoned their horse and were immediately cut down by the rebels.

Simon and his men mercilessly slaughtered the soldiers, who were unable to escape the rift or retreat. Meanwhile, the archers continued pelting them from above. The stalled army didn't have a chance and couldn't defend themselves much less create an offense against the hidden rebel army. One after another, they died in a blood bath that they had expected to be reaping against the rebels.

It went on for more than two hours, the rift turned to a killing field. When the bodies were so numerous that living Romans couldn't move forward in a belated attempt to attack them, and all the arrows had been shot, Simon and his fighters quickly abandoned the valley, mounted their awaiting horses and rode away. They escaped without a single casualty.

Marcellus sat on his horse expressionless as he listened to the screams of his men echoing from deep within the passage. Simon had cleverly twisted the general's own trap to kill him and the rest of the rebels. Now, he'd lost a substantial share of his own troops. Only a couple of dozen soldiers managed to find their way back to the entrance and they did so on foot, leaving their trapped horses behind.

When it was over, Marcellus and his aides gingerly rode through a scattering of bodies that littered the rift valley. When they reached the far side, blood was streaming along the path. He pulled up short and gasped at the sight of hundreds and hundreds of dead and wounded soldiers that cluttered and blocked the rift. He turned his horse around with his stomach churning.

All he could think about was what Hadrian would say about this failed incursion. Maybe he could cover it up somehow. The problem was there were too many surviving soldiers who would know what happened and the emperor would insist on an inquiry.

As they rode into Ein Gedi, Simon and Levi were both surprised to see a camp already set up at the oasis. How did Rubin and the recruits do it so fast? He wondered. In addition, there were more soldiers. They seemed too many, he thought, recalling the ones he'd sent ahead. Where did they come from? Then, he saw Ruth and Rubin standing near several rabbis. He dismounted and was met by a warm hug from Ruth. "I'm so glad you've made it. I was so worried. Was it terrible?"

"It was for them!"

"That's good. We've got a surprise for you. Turn around."

He looked back and couldn't believe his eyes. "Noah! You're alive!" He shouted in shock as they both hugged each other, then Levi stepped up and punched Noah lovingly on the shoulder. "Now I know how this camp was set up so quickly. Noah was already here," Levi said and they hugged.

Simon sensed a heaviness hanging over Noah and knew he had a story to tell. Noah met his gaze and said: "I'll tell you all about it this evening and I want to hear what happened up in that rift."

We all would gather, relax and talk tonight, but not celebrate, Simon thought. We *would* celebrate when the Romans were finally driven out of Israel. Besides, we would need to be ready in case the Romans regrouped and came after us. Yet, he didn't think that would happen, at least not for the time being. They were too overwhelmed and in disarray by their massive losses in the rift to even wonder where the rebels had fled. He would send out scouts tomorrow, and he predicted the remains of the legion would be retreating.

That evening, torches burned throughout the camp and rebel soldiers patrolled the perimeter. Simon and Ruth, his generals, and the rabbis finished their dinner of bread, cooked vegetable with dried beef and dates, and now they were enjoying glasses of wine.

Simon noticed Noah's troubled expression and knew that he was getting ready to tell his story. He encouraged him to begin. "I know you probably don't want to talk about what happened, but we need to hear it, Noah."

"I know. It was terrible. We saw the fire on the mountains and immediately abandoned our encampment outside Hebron. We headed for Jerusalem and were south of Bethlehem when we were attacked from two sides by legions, at least two of them. The Romans quickly surrounded us."

Noah paused and his head hung before he continued. "We fought hard but we never had a chance. We were losing troops by the hundreds, then thousands. He looked over at Simon, tears in his eyes. He cleared his throat. "I didn't surrender. But when we were down to about two thousand remaining and the Romans continued their slaughter, I spread the word for everyone to withdraw." He shook his head, "But…"

"Go on," Simon said. No one was drinking their wine now.

Noah nodded, wiped the back of his hand across his eyes. "But they didn't let us go. They pursued us, trapped us, and we lost even more. But so did they. Finally, we got away from them. But by then, we were down to five hundred and some. We fled here to Ein Gedi."

"Five hundred fortunate souls," Akiva said. "Thank you, Noah. You did the right thing."

"Did I, Simon? Or should we have continued fighting and killing Romans?"

"Akiva is right," Simon said. "You did all that you could do. You saved five hundred lives."

"And they're here now," Noah responded. "Thank you for understanding."

"There's something else," Simon said and his gaze slowly slid across all those assembled. "Shortly after I sent Noah and half the army to Hebron, the Romans attacked Jerusalem while the city was vulnerable. There's the question of the timing of the attacks on Jerusalem and the troops in Judea."

No one said anything. "I know many of you are thinking it wasn't a good move on my part to send out half the army. But it could've been an excellent one to bring our troops from Hebron in behind the Romans before they attacked Jerusalem. But it didn't work that way because they knew we were vulnerable in Jerusalem and they knew where the rest of the army was located. Someone told them."

"A spy?" Akiva uttered.

"Most likely a mere coincidence," Rabbi Palmer said. "I may have my differences with you, Simon, but I didn't think you were fearful of your own people."

"All good leaders have a healthy dose of suspicion," he responded.

Palmer didn't respond.

"No matter. I will discover who the traitor is and he will be dealt with accordingly."

After an awkward silence, Akiva changed the subject. "Well, Noah sadly told us what happened in the field. Now, Simon, please tell us the good news about the battle today in the valley. I understand it was very one-sided."

Simon smiled at Levi. "You can begin."

Levi laughed. "And you can finish just as you finished off our enemy today."

Chapter 16

It was bedtime in the emperor's palace. Hadrian was standing in his ante chamber where his manservant was dressing him for bed. He was so used to the nightly procedure that he had two manservants available each evening in case one was ill. Both of his current ones were relatively new and young, in their twenties, just the way he liked them.

This one, Elon, was being trained in how to prepare Hadrian for the empress on the one day a week when they had their conjugal visit. Truthfully, he enjoyed the prepping sessions with his youthful manservants far more than the bedroom dalliances with Sabina. If he didn't break away immediately and go to Sabina, she would be disappointed. He could only hold on so long.

"Go on now." Hadrian flicked his hand sending Elon out of the room.

He walked into the bedroom ready for her and stopped when he saw her sitting in her antechamber while her favorite attendant brushed her hair. "I'm ready, Sabina," he called out from the foot of the bed.

She stood up, dismissed her attendant, and walked over to him. "Not tonight. I'm not feeling so well. Something I ate."

He knew he could do anything he wanted with her and she would abide by him. It didn't matter how she felt. That was the way it was. He was emperor. But he was already losing interest and she noticed. Without another word, they both crawled into the huge bed. Sabina blew out the three candles on her side but Hadrian let his burn. His mind was already drifting to his meeting earlier in the day.

"General Severus didn't even ask about the health of my 'children' today."

After a few moments, she responded. "I thought you were annoyed when he did?"

He ignored her comment. "The inability to kill this Judean leader is really trying my patience."

"What did he tell you?"

"That General Marcellus is returning with more bad news. I'll see him tomorrow and he better have a good explanation of why Simon, Son of Star, is still breathing. I want the head of that so-called messiah, not some excuses."

"What would you do with his head, Hadrian?" Her voice started to slur as she drifted off.

"I would hold it up for the senators to see. Maybe that would make some of them think twice about defying me."

Sabina didn't answer. Her back was turned to him and he listened to her slow deep breaths. Then, he blew out his candles.

The next morning, Hadrian sat on his curule seat on his raised platform in front of the senate. General Severus and General Marcellus stood in front of him. Marcellus stared straight ahead looking like a condemned man, Hadrian thought.

Severus turned to face the assembled group. "The senate meeting is now called to order." The room fell silent. Hadrian waited for the next part of the statement about the emperor's children and the army being in good health, but again it never came.

"What do my generals have for me?"

"Your Majesty, Simon bar Kochva escaped our legions."

"What does that name mean, General?"

"I believe it is Simon, Son of Star. He is considered the Judean messiah."

"I'm well aware. What is his real name?"

Marcellus hesitated. "I'm not sure."

"It's Simon ben Kosevah. He is a human and vulnerable to the sword. Like anyone else."

All eyes were on Hadrian as this information sank in. He felt the pressure and judgment from them. Hadrian glared at General Marcellus. "How is that possible? How did he escape?"

"His men trapped us in a valley near the Dead Sea." Marcellus sounded as defeated as he looked.

"His men who numbered in the thousands?"

"No, Your Majesty. A few hundred."

Hadrian flashed a curious look at Severus who blankly stared into nothingness. The Emperor loomed over Marcellus. "How many men have we lost?"

"Hard to tell until—"

"How many?" Hadrian shouted.

Marcellus took a deep breath and finally let it out. "Over two thousand."

Hadrian's stare penetrated Marcellus. "You have failed me, General. Worse. You have embarrassed me, yourself, and all of Rome. You have failed the empire."

Marcellus' eyes were vacant as he looked up at his Emperor. Hadrian stood up and extended his hand, palm up. "Your sword, General."

Marcellus dutifully unsheathed his sword and handed it to the emperor.

Hadrian turned it over in his hand, looking at it as if admiring the craftsmanship. "Nice weapon. One fit for a leader."

He glowered at Marcellus. "But not for you." With that, he ran the point of the blade into Marcellus' chest, killing him instantly. The senators gasped as the general slid off the blade, and crumpled to the floor.

Hadrian's gaze fell onto Severus. "You are the last of my three most trusted generals. Take half of my army, reclaim Judea, kill this so-called messiah, and don't fail me."

"That will leave many provinces vulnerable, Your Majesty."

Hadrian considered the general's comment. "What is the current status of those

Provinces?"

Severus looked uncomfortable. "Word has it that they've heard of Simon's victories."

"And?"

"Our hold on them is weakening."

"Then, they are already vulnerable. The only way to secure them now is to kill Simon bar Kochva."

Severus gave the emperor a quick bow. "Yes, Your Majesty." He spun on a heel and marched away.

"And General," Hadrian called after him.

Severus paused and faced the emperor.

"Do not fail me." He met Severus's gaze, then glanced down at Marcellus's body.

The general nodded and quickly left the building.

Hadrian scanned the room with narrowed eyes. Everyone averted their gaze.

He smirked at their discomfort.

That evening, Hadrian found no joy in his dinner of rabbit, bean soup, vegetables, bread and cheese prepared by the best chef in Rome. He spent the entire meal going over the events of the day in detail with Sabina. Now, he was on his second vessel of wine and was pondering the stability of the empire with so many legions of troops headed towards Judea.

"Just relax, Hadrian. General Severus will handle this."

"It's costing us a lot of men. This Simon is the only one to defeat our legions in a hundred years. It's affecting our ability to recruit more men. They don't want to be sent to Judea.

He stood up and ambled over to a table covered in Roman coins. He scooped up a fistful of them. Opening his fist, they flowed out of his hand, leaving only a few. They were properly stamped Roman coins with Hadrian's likeness on them. Nearby was a small pile of coins over-stamped with Simon's image. He picked up a couple and studied them. Below, Simon's likeness is written, *Simon, President of Israel.*

He took another gulp of wine and frowned. "He is not only funding his rebellion with stolen Roman currency, but he is erasing our currency and my image from the pages of history. What legacy would I have left behind, if any?"

"Hadrian, you will be remembered as one of the best emperors ever," Sabina said. "You care for your people. You have visited all of your provinces and improved their lives. You have strengthened the empire. But now…"

He angrily tossed the coins onto the table. They bounced off and clattered to the stone floor. "Severus says I'm weakening the empire by sending more troops to Judea."

Sabina stood and faced him. "It's true that this campaign against one man is having an adverse effect on the entire empire."

"That can't be denied."

"Then, should you continue it?"

He clenched his fists. "It will be far worse for the empire if I stop now. We will be admitting defeat. It could threaten our hold on all our land."

"Hadrian, this Simon, he is thousands of miles away. If you let him get into your head, then he will have defeated Rome without ever leaving Judea."

She turned and walked to the bedroom, leaving Hadrian to ponder her words.

Chapter 17

Simon walked through his army, watching the training in progress. His generals: Noah, Levi, and Rubin followed him. Soldiers glanced over at them or stopped what they were doing and saluted. He watched his captains instructing and demonstrating battle techniques and stopped to talk whenever he noticed how a captain could improve his training procedures or better deal with his soldiers. He wanted his captains to be strict but fair, especially with the new recruits.

Several months had passed since the victory in the rift valley. Once Simon had confirmed that the battered legion had retreated and returned to their stronghold in Caesarea, he talked with the village leaders in Ein Gedi. They despised the Romans and were behind the rebels. But many of the families did not want their boys to join the rebel's cause and that had angered Simon. A year earlier, after he had been turned away from En Gedi, he had written letters to the governor of the village complaining about the lack of willingness by the men of Ein Gedi to join the rebels. Now, the governor told Simon that he was welcome to use the village as a base as long as villagers were not required to join the rebels. Simon accepted the concession in order to establish their base at the prosperous village. At that point, Simon believed the rebels had months, maybe a year, before the Romans mounted another offensive. In that time, he vowed to build a huge army, protect the village in any way he could, and prepare for the inevitable.

Meanwhile, he wanted to make everything as familiar to Ruth as possible during the months of re-building the rebel force. So when the governor of Ein Gedi offered a house for Simon and Ruth, he readily agreed. They lived a life that was as normal as possible under the circumstances. He would like to marry her, raise a family, and farm the land. But the desire to free Israel was a bigger calling and he knew he had to sacrifice his desires for a peaceful family life.

In spite of its desert location west of the Dead Sea, Ein Gedi was a lush oasis with date palms and balsam trees from which expensive medicines were made. The troop encampment on the outskirts of the village was pleasant in comparison to their previous training encampment on the foothills of Mount Nebo. Perhaps, the appeal of the oasis location made it easier for Simon to attract new recruits. He had sent out his experienced rebels to villages and cities to enlist new soldiers. He'd also returned to the rift valley with a hundred soldiers, where they'd gathered weapons and equipment left behind by the Romans they'd slaughtered. Dealing with the slowly decaying bodies of soldiers and horses was a difficult task and even the toughest battle-hardened soldiers were sickened by what they encountered. Back in Ein Gedi, surviving Roman horses turned up for several weeks, adding to their stables.

Words spread about the victory against the Romans and the need for new recruits. Soon, volunteers began arriving, first a dozen or so each week, then hundreds. One week, more than nine hundred arrived and the troop numbers were steadily growing. They were all accommodated with tents in the camp, supplied with weapons and entered into Simon's training program. Now, tens of thousands of soldiers were training daily and many of them thought he was the messiah as well as a military leader.

"Thousands of Samaritans have joined our cause," Levi mentioned proudly as they passed by a battalion of them.

"What about the Christians?"

They hesitated to answer and Simon glared at them.

"Still no Christians among the recruits."

"What about the Christians right here in the villages, in Judea? I thought we were making progress with them."

"We were with the younger ones, but the priests have forbidden them from joining our fight. He told them they would be ex-communicated and even forbidden to return home."

Simon angrily stalked off.

Once a week, a fish, meat and vegetable market was held in Ein Gedi, and Ruth liked to arrive early for the best selections. Sometimes the offerings were plentiful, other times, they were meager. Today, everything goat-related was in abundance – meat, cheese, milk – and she was picking out cheese when she heard her name called and looked up to see a familiar face moving her way among the shoppers.

"Mary! Is that really you?" Ruth dropped the cloth bag with the cheese, rushed forward and hugged her. "You came!"

"I said I would."

"Was it difficult to get away?"

Mary looked around. "I want to tell you all about it, but not here."

A few minutes later, the two long-time friends were seated at a table in Ruth's house. Simon had left at dawn. "After I received the message from you, all I wanted to do was to get out of the capital," Mary began. "My papa warned me it was dangerous but that he would help me find a way."

"He agreed that you should leave?"

"Oh, he thought it was for the best. He said he would miss me dearly but he wanted me to be safe, and the best thing to do was get out of Jerusalem."

Ruth nodded and smiled. "You can stay with us for as long as you like. I'm very thankful that your father let me stay with you all those years. You can also help me when I get bigger," she said, touching her belly. "I'm with child."

"Oh, Ruth. Why didn't you tell me immediately?" She got up and hugged her. "Congratulations. Did you tell Simon? What did he say?"

"I just realized it the other day. I haven't told him yet. Don't say anything yet. I don't want him to worry."

"I promise I won't."

"Now tell me, Mary, how did you get out? It must've been frightening."

"It was all planned. But it was still scary. Papa saw that the guards didn't check the carts driven by Romans. I left with two teen boys who wanted to join the rebel army. We hid in a cart driven by a Roman and headed for Caesarea. But the boys overpowered him, clubbed him on the head, and took over the cart when we were outside of Jerusalem."

Mary went on to tell her about things in Jerusalem, most of which Ruth had already heard from Simon, whose spies easily infiltrated life in the capital. The spies also carried messages back and forth, including ones that Ruth and Mary had sent.

"The Romans control everything in the city. They mostly leave us alone except for anyone preaching and even studying the Torah. If they're caught, they are killed. They still try to convert us to believe in their pagan gods but to no avail. Oh, and of course, they are still hunting for anyone connected to the rebels."

"That goes without saying," Ruth said.

"So far, they haven't connected my father with the rebels."

"But he was just involved with arranging the supplies."

"He never said much about what he was doing. But the supplies were all stolen from the Roman's storage buildings. They included caches of gold and silver coins."

"Oh, I didn't know your father was involved in that operation. As Simon likes to say, the Romans have kept the rebel army fed, clothed and armed."

"I'm proud of him. But worried, too," Mary said. "If someone in that group is caught and tortured, he could be exposed."

"He should leave."

She shook her head. "He won't. He's committed to staying and spying for the cause."

"He's very brave, and I can understand why he would want you to get out. I hope you will like it here."

"It looks wonderful from what I've seen."

"It's ideal if I wear blinders."

"What do you mean?"

She motioned with her hand at the house and her garden. "This is most likely temporary; things were bound to change and maybe soon. I want marriage and a family but Simon is hesitant. He says he wants to wait until we've driven the Romans out of Israel."

"How long will that be?"

"Exactly what I asked him but he couldn't tell me."

"I don't blame you for being frustrated, Ruth, but you knew who he was and what he does before you met him."

She met Mary's gaze. "I know what he does. But I've never known who he is."

"What do you mean? You don't think he is the messiah?"

"I don't know, Mary. They say he is our savior, our messiah, but I know him as a man."

"Has he ever told you that he's the messiah?"

"No. But he doesn't deny it either."

Simon, Levi and Rubin along with several of Simon's soldiers approached a house in a village, half a day away from Ein Gedi. Simon requested to see the village priest and one of the villagers guided them to the house.. He peered through an open window and saw a gathering of men sitting in a circle on a large area rug. The priest, a tall gaunt man with long stringy hair, was standing and leading a prayer session.

"Our Lord, Jesus, though rejected and put to death, is the true messiah. We await his return."

The men in the circle made the sign of the cross – touching their foreheads, hearts and shoulders. At that moment, a torch sailed through the open window and landed in their midst, igniting the rug. The men shouted as they bolted to their feet and out of the house where they were met by Simon and his men, who beat them with sticks as they came out the door. The terrified men collapsed and cowered.

"Who among you is the leader?" Simon asked.

They pointed at the priest without hesitation and Simon grabbed him by the throat.

"This is what you will suffer at the hands of the Romans if you do not join us in our fight! The Romans will come with swords, not sticks! Do you understand?"

"We have but only one messiah," the priest sputtered as he tried to breathe and talk at the same time. "Our lord is Jesus Christ, and we will not fight in the name of any other proclaimed messiah."

Simon bristled with anger and threw the man into the dirt. "It is your chance to avenge your messiah. The Romans killed him. By the way, he was from Israel, a Judean like us!"

"Fighting for a false messiah does not avenge anything. The real messiah, Jesus Christ, was the son of God! He did not go around chopping people's heads off!"

Simon glared at the priest. "Then, you will soon be learning how to pray to the Roman gods or die, maybe on a cross."

Once a week, Akiva rode for two hours from Ein Gedi to a mountain cave where his favorite student Shimon bar Yochai meditated and wrote. Wisdom was flowing through Shimon and he wrote as fast as he could on a scroll perched on a low table. Their roles had been reversed. Instead of the student serving the master, Akiva carried food and water to Shimon to keep him fortified. He knew that his long-time student was producing a spiritual masterpiece for the ages. Shimon called it the Zohar and it was the mystical roots of the holy biblical scriptures that expanded on the writings of mystics from a thousand years earlier.

Akiva entered the cave and followed a narrow passage that led to a roomy cavern with a high ceiling. Shimon had been guided here, an affirmation that he was on the correct path. He felt that he was in the hands of a higher force. He was seated on a rug in front of the low table where he was writing on a long parchment scroll, just as he was, last week, when Akiva visited him. Next to the table was a sleeping pad stuffed with straw and covered by a light blanket. "Rashbi, have you gotten up and gone outside for a walk and fresh air today?"

"Master, there's no time. The knowledge and wisdom are flowing through me and I must capture it or maybe lose it."

"I understand, but you must maintain your health. You are very thin."

"What I'm doing is more important."

"I've meditated on your work and I too received an inspired knowledge."

Shimon laid down his iron writing instrument that used a combination of lead and silicone metals to produce even green lines. Then he turned his attention to Akiva.

"What you are writing will be hidden for many generations. Only in the distant future will a time come when the spiritual wisdom of the Zohar will be needed to remove darkness from the earth and bring in well-being and blessings to mankind. It's good that you are writing in Aramaic rather than Hebrew. Few would understand it, least of all, the Romans."

Shimon frowned. "That may be so. Yet, the knowledge applies to this time as well. I am connected to an upper force that is bestowing and giving. It's the opposite of the need to control and rule people that we see in the Romans. But, the opposition is very destructive as well. We need to break away from the hatred and become more like the upper force and the connection to the source of all that exists. We are all one desire that was created by the upper force. That desire is to enjoy."

"I understand, Rashbi. But we also live in the physical world where there is joy and hate."

"Yes, it's true. The one desire was shattered into thousands of pieces and that is our individual souls. The emphasis becomes the individual and we see others who are not like us as enemies. Rather than to hate, we need to come together, to unite as one again. We have a choice to pursue the path of suffering or the path of light. As we enter an advanced state, we can reach beyond the path of suffering. That is what the heart of the Zohar is about."

Akiva was tempted to tell Shimon that what he was saying was fine if you were living in a cave away from the outside world. Yet, he knew deep down in his heart that what Shimon was saying was correct and wise. As the rabbi of the rebels, he was living in both worlds. He understood Shimon's connection with the upper force and the desire to remain in that realm. But, he also knew that the path of suffering was nearly upon them again, and he feared it would end in a very bad way.

Simon stood alone on a low hill from where he could see thousands of rebel troops engaging in fake sword fights. He knew that many of them were bored with the training and were in need of the real deal; to combat. They'd been training for months and wanted to kill. It wouldn't be long, he thought. All morning, he could feel a dark energy building, like a pressure inside his head, and he recognized it as the legions marching their way towards them. In his mind, he heard the pounding of hoofs that rumbled the earth. He knew the Romans were on the move, coming for them.

In the past, he'd been excited by every confrontation with the Romans, but this time, it felt more like a duty and he knew that no matter what the outcome, many of his soldiers would die on the battlefield. More and more, he was plagued by questions of his role and abilities. If he were really the messiah, wouldn't he have the ability to turn the Romans around and send them back to Rome? Send them all back to Rome and create a country where there are no threats, sufferings, bloodshed or destruction, and everyone lived in peace.

A part of him, now long buried, didn't want the responsibilities that he had undertaken in building and leading the rebel army, and especially by accepting the role of the messiah. At weaker moments, he thought about what a different life he would lead if he and Ruth fled Israel, maybe for Greece. But that wasn't going to happen. He was committed to his country, to the fight against the Romans, no matter the cost.

He pushed those thoughts away and focused on his favorite brigade, the ones that he had trained himself. The brigade consisted of three hundred fully armored spear fighters. Following the path of the Spartans, they trained in tight phalanxes with each soldier armed with a long shield from chin to knee, brass breastplate and helmets. They were lined up now shoulder-to-shoulder behind their shields with their spear aimed forward over the top of the shields. They marched forward at the direction of their captains. Simon had taught the phalanxes to work as a cohesive group that included an abbreviated second line. If any soldiers fell in battle, a soldier from the second line would quickly replace the fallen one.

Master Leon had taught Simon the phalanx technique. At the time, Simon never thought he would be leading an army one day. Since he had been trained as an individual, he'd learned a variety spear-fighting techniques, including how to overcome an opponent who had gotten too close to allow the spear to be effective. Because of his own individualized training, he taught the same techniques to his battalion. They appreciated the dual training of phalanx and sole spear fighter.

One of the sub-brigades was practicing spear fighting in pairs and he immediately noticed improper techniques, the sort of movements that Leon would've instantly corrected after first responding with a deadly thrust. He slowly descended the hill, taking his time not wanting to disrupt the training. But, everyone had seen him and the soldiers nearest to the hill immediately stopped what they were doing and turned their attention to him.

He waved a hand to the captains telling them to continue with the training. He kept walking until he reached the spear-bearing brigade. The soldiers stopped at his approach and he called them all over. "You are all working well together in the phalanx. You're a team, a single unit, and a giant armored caterpillar. But the individual fighting techniques need some work."

He walked over and motioned to a tall muscular soldier to come forward. Simon pulled out his knife and pointed it at the soldier. "You come at me with your spear."

"I don't want to hurt you. You're not wearing an armor and you don't have a spear."

"Just come at me."

The brawny soldier raised his spear to slash downward, but Simon instantly moved in close, blocked his arm and jabbed the knife point under the soldier's jaw. "You're dead. Don't start with a slash, for it opens you up. A spear is like a knife; it is better to thrust than slash. Let me borrow your sword."

Simon dismissed the soldier and pointed to another one. A short, stocky soldier stepped forward with his spear. Like the other one, he wore bronze chest armor and a helmet. "Come at me with a thrust."

He did so, but Simon quickly stepped to the side and slashed his sword against the soldier's helmet. "Do you know why I was able to slash and hit your head?"

"Yeah, because you're Simon!" he said and adjusted his cock-eyed helmet.

The soldiers, who were grouped around them, laughed. So did Simon. "I do have more experience than you. But the reason I'm looking for is the position of your spear after your thrust. You let it down exposing your head. Keep the tip up at eye level and the way to do that is lower your back hand to your hip."

"I thought you told us to have the back hand by the arm pit."

"That's how you finish a long thrust. But you need to keep your tip even with your eyes. All thrusts should start with the back hand by the hip. As you complete your thrust, you then lower the back hand to the hip so the tip goes up and protects your head."

Simon looked up to see a rider galloping hard towards the camp and as he drew closer, he recognized him as one of his scouts. Noah intercepted him and the scout pointed to the north and waved his hands. Simon couldn't hear what he was saying, but he knew what it was about.

Chapter 18

Noah was looking over a map of Judea that was spread out on a table when Simon, Levi and Rubin arrived. The rabbis and several captains were present. "What do we have?" Simon asked.

Noah touches the map to the North of Judea. "Our scout reported that he had spotted the Roman legions in the north of Judea and they are two days out at most."

"How many?"

"Hard to tell, but he said it could be as many as ten."

All except Simon reacted in shock. He was expecting as much. "Quiet! Quiet! I want every man to the north of the city. We ride out at dawn."

"Ride to where?" Rabbi Elazar asked.

Simon regarded him as if he was an idiot. "North. To engage the Romans of course, uncle."

"Going against ten legions will be suicide."

Simon ignored him and addressed Noah. "Everyone to the North. We ride at dawn."

"Yes, My Lord."

Within the hour, the encampment was buzzing with activity as soldiers prepared their armor and weapons for battle. As Simon walked through the camp, excited soldiers gathered with their friends and some shouted with glee that the time to fight was finally here. Simon looked at the young faces knowing that it might be their last day on earth.

Akiva had come back from his recent visit to Shimon, his scholarly student who lived in a cave, with a message. *We may be righteous in our fight but we are on a path of suffering.* Shimon supposedly talked to God… or God talked to him. If that's what God told him, then Simon didn't need that kind of help. Scholars who live in caves had a very different view of the world than a military leader. He wanted God to tell him that he was on a path of victory. He knew he was doing the right thing and at great personal cost. The same could be said for his troops.

The sun was rising. Thousands of mounted men were spread across the desert. Simon was perched on his horse in front of them. He turned to the nearest troops and shouted his message so as many soldiers as possible could hear him.

"Though we have suffered casualties against the Romans, we have taken far more lives than we have lost." Repeaters among the troops called out his message so everyone could hear it. "We will ride out and engage them in the desert." He listened to his words being repeated, then continued: "Where the dirt and soil will run red with their blood and their bodies will bake in the sun." His words were echoed again. "Their bones will forever be a warning to any and all who dares to challenge the people of Israel."

Cheers from the mounted troops rippled across the desert. Simon trotted along the edge of the troops inspecting them. He noticed a slender teen, probably a recent recruit, who was shaking and quietly weeping. He moved next to him, took his reins, and led him to the rear. "You stay back here with the medics. You'll do fine." He signaled one of the medics. "This soldier is going to be your assistant. You tell him what to do."

The boy still looked distraught but managed a smile and thanked Simon. As Simon turned away, he saw the rabbis standing off to one side. Rabbi Akiva waved to him and looked thrilled. In comparison, Elazar and Palmer looked discontented. Simon spotted Ruth and Mary, who stood near the rabbis and trotted over to them. Their faces were etched with concern. Tears rolled down Ruth's cheeks.

"Don't worry. We'll hold our own. Mary, thank you again for coming. Please stay with Ruth and both of you stay strong. And stay out of the way!"

He looked over at the rabbis and shouted. "We will make the Romans regret they ever heard the name -- Simon, Son of Star!"

That was enough for Rabbi Elazar. He exploded with rage. "You arrogant fool! You elevate yourself and take all the credit! It is God who has given you the wings of victory, God alone!"

"I have kept this land free in the face of the biggest empire the world has ever known. I will continue to do so with or without God's help!"

"That's sacrilege! Your over-confidence and hubris will be your downfall!" Elazar snapped.

Simon turned to his nearest captain. "Take this Rabbi away from me before

I cut him down!"

Before the captain could act, Ruth gently led the frail rabbi away. Simon accepted Ruth's handling of the situation and rode back to the front of the troops. He was annoyed by Elazar's outspoken criticism just as the battle approached but it only made him even more forward to the combat. "Let's go find where they are hiding!" he shouted and galloped off and his troops thundered after him.

Severus and Clavius rode side by side at the front of the Roman war machine, composed of tens of thousands of armored and armed soldiers, some pulling siege weapons across the desert. The Roman flags held high whipped in the wind. Clavius had never seen anything so impressive in his life. He reveled in the power of the Roman military might. He expected a tough battle but the rebels didn't have a chance. Even more troops were on the way. The rebellion would soon be over. He glanced at the general and felt proud that he had emerged as not only a member of Severus's entourage but as his right-hand man, at least for now. He fully expected the general to order him into the battle.

Clavius narrowed his gaze, focusing on something in the distance. "My Lord, the horizon..."

A cloud of dust clung to the desert floor in a narrow but lengthy line. A slowly growing rumble accompanied it.

"I know, I know, it's Simon and his rebels," Severus said.

Clavius immediately leaped into action, raising his sword and shouting: "The enemy approaches! Prepare for battle!"

A wave of activity flowed through the masses as weapons of all sorts were readied.

"Onward!" Severus shouted, and moments later the army began stampeding past the general and his entourage. He turned to Clavius. "Go find Simon. Kill him!"

Simon led the charge; his generals close behind. Thirty thousand troops followed, thundering across the desert, closing the distance between them and the Romans. Simon knew they were outnumbered but he was counting on his troops being faster and more adept. They were also more dedicated to the cause since the rebels were fighting for their own country and the Romans were far from home, engaged against an enemy that knew the territory and was intent on defending it.

Both massive armies collided and engaged each other in a tangled fray as battle cries rose, followed by screams of pain. Simon's spear brigade dismounted as planned and formed a tight line near the front, shoulder-to-shoulder with their long shields and spears. The Romans at first seemed baffled by the formation and rode around it. Finally, one Roman soldier broke up the brigade by charging his large horse through the shield-bearing soldiers. Other riders followed, galloping their steads between the shielded soldiers who had no time to respond other than to move aside as quickly as possible. In spite of their attempts to reinstate their wall of resistance, the spear-bearing soldiers were soon fighting individually instead of as a cohesive unit.

The clanging of swords against spears, and swords against swords, created a shrieking metallic raucous. Arrows showered down from both sides. Blood spouted from fatal wounds for seconds before soldiers toppled off to the ground. The fallen and injured were quickly trampled and crushed, assuring that few would survive even minor wounds if they fell to the battlefield.

Once in the midst of the Romans, Simon abandoned his horse and turned into a killing machine, taking on more than one Roman at a time and cutting them down one after another. He danced, dodged, and vaulted as he slew Roman after Roman. His generals followed his lead, staying close to him, taking on multiple enemy soldiers and helping each other when one was overwhelmed. Blood flowed and the cries of the injured and dying, along with the whinnies of horses, the clash of swords, and the stomping of hoofs. Hundreds on each side died within the early going and horses without riders clogged the battlefield.

Clavius remained on his horse to make better use of his size. He galloped towards a rebel but remained outside the reach of the man's sword. Then, leaning over and taking advantage of the momentum of his horse, he executed a quick, powerful swing of his sword which cleanly removed the rebel's head. Satisfied, he watched the headless body wobble and fall, landing next to the head which stared sightlessly toward the sky.

Not all of his kills were so clean and quick but they were easy. He looked for the smaller, younger inexperienced soldiers – soldiers in name only – and took them down one after another. He thought of it as a sport.

There was no question that they would win and decimate the rebels. If not today, then soon. There were so many legions coming that no opponent anywhere in the world would have a chance against the Romans.

He spotted Simon fighting on foot and watched as he slaughtered one Roman after another. Here was his chance, he thought. He would charge into the fray while Simon was occupied with two or more soldiers. He could stick him in the back and drive his sword right through his heart. There would be witnesses and no one would doubt that he was the messiah killer.

Doing so would impress General Severus and bring him great honor. It would make up for his failure the first time he confronted Simon in Jerusalem. And the death of the messiah would signal the end of the rebellion. But then, Clavius noticed the toughened soldiers around Simon who were as capable as any of Roman's best. No doubt they were Simon's top fighters. He was no fool. Killing Simon and dying himself in the process was no victory, not for him. He quickly backed away and decided to let other Romans take on the rebel leader. Maybe one would get a lucky strike.

Out of the corner of his eye, he spotted a rebel charging him from the side. He ducked at the last moment and the soldier's sword bounced off his helmet. Another rebel rushed at him from the opposite side, and again, the long reach of his sword paid off. The tip of his blade swiped across the soldier's throat and hot blood spurted onto him. Clavius twisted to the other side, expecting a second attack from the other soldier who had struck his helmet. But the other rebel had smartly moved on. Moments later, though Clavius spotted him in another pitched sword fight. He charged forward and slammed his sword down onto the rebel's helmet with such force that he broke his neck. The rebel toppled off his horse, dead before he hit the ground.

Hit me in the helmet, will you? Clavius muttered and rode on.

Simon thrust his sword under the chest armor of an attacking Roman, gutting him, and spilling his intestines. He quickly turned at the sound of a horse galloping right at him. He raised his sword but held back at the last moment as the rider reined in and Simon saw it was a rebel soldier, one of his scouts.

"My Lord!" the young scout shouted. "The Romans are coming from the land and sea. Legions upon legions. The port is jammed with troop ships and more are waiting to enter." Noah ran up, having overheard. "What now, My Lord?"

Simon smirked in satisfaction. "This is great news. We have been victorious."

Noah threw him a perplexed look. "This is victory?"

"Whenever your enemy has to throw everything they've got at you, you have them frightened, and fear is victory." After a moment, he added. "Nonetheless, we'll withdraw."

Noah nodded, quickly mounted his horse and rode off, shouting: "Withdraw! Withdraw!" Other soldiers repeated the order as they turned and retreated from the battlefield.

Within minutes, thousands of rebel soldiers were galloping away. A few rebels broke away from sword fights and were pursued. But Simon, Levi, and Rubin caught up to the Romans that were chasing rebels and cut them down with slashes to their necks and backs.

Still feeling the effects of the sword that struck his helmet, Clavius walked about the battlefield with a rebel spear that he'd recovered and jammed the tip into the torso of every wounded rebel lying on the ground or sitting up. Other Romans joined him, hacking away at the wounded enemy. Meanwhile, medics attended to or carted away wounded Romans. The first battle was over, and Clavius cursed himself now for not having the courage to confront Simon on the field.

Chapter 19

The rebel troops returned to their camp by late afternoon. Even though the battle lasted only three hours, it was intense and bloody. Now, the medics began attending to the injured who were able to ride back to the camp. Some literally slumped and fell from their horses when they arrived.

Simon made a quick inspection and estimated that he'd lost at least fifteen hundred soldiers in the fray. After his assessment, he called his general and captains together and told them his plans. Some looked startled, others dazed when they heard they would be abandoning Ein Gedi within a couple of hours. Then he told them to join him and they rode into the village square where worried residents were gathered. Ruth, Mary, and several rabbis emerge from a nearby building.

Simon raised a hand and everyone turned to hear what he had to say. "Attention residents of Ein Gedi and others who are here in support of our rebellion against the Roman domination of Israel." He addressed the crowd in his usual commanding voice. "Though we have delivered a decisive blow to the Roman army, more legions will arrive soon. Like Jerusalem, this village will become impossible to defend and fighting will just thin our numbers. We need a stronghold that will be extremely difficult for Rome to breach. Therefore, we will move to the mountain village of Beitar where its elevated fortress-like structure will give us a distinct advantage. We will leave for the village within hours.

He paused and looked over the distressed residents. "You can join us in Beitar or you can remain here and hope for the best. For those who want to leave, I am assigning a trusted general and a team of soldiers to guard and guide you to the village." He looked over to his generals. "Rubin, are you willing?"

"Of course, My Lord."

"Good. Pick two captains who can each select fifty soldiers to serve as guards for the residents. The first thing to do is work with the villagers to collect all the food that can be found, and empty all the coffers. The villagers will be separated from the troops. If we encounter any resistance in our trek, it will be against the army, not the villagers."

A flurry of activity ensued as everyone leaped into action to prepare to vacate the village. Ruth ran up to Simon. "You know, I'm going with you. I knew we wouldn't be staying here."

"Of course you are going to Beitar. Rubin, take care of Ruth and her friend, Mary. They are your primary concern along with everyone else leaving the village."

"Why can't we go with you, Simon?"

"Because I'll be with the troops in case we are attacked."

Ruth nodded but didn't look pleased. "We'll be crossing the desert and going into the mountains in the dark."

"There's a full moon tonight. It will be safer that way. It's not very likely that the Romans will be looking for a fight in the middle of the night. They'll be asleep in their tents. Besides, we can't wait until morning. They'll be ready to attack."

"He's right," Mary said. "It's better to make the journey at night."

"Maybe so." Ruth managed a smile. "At least we'll be together."

Noah moved alongside Simon as they trotted their horses back to the encampment.

"Why did we take Jerusalem and Hebron if we were only going to abandon them?"

Simon looked over at him. Maybe because he was older than Simon, Noah rarely addressed him as 'My Lord.' But Simon had come to accept him for what he was. He knew Noah was loyal and a strong leader of the men who respected him. "Rome didn't care when we took the small villages. But the cities were a matter of pride to them. We have freed Israel from their clutches for three years, Noah. They couldn't let that stand, and taking them back has cost them dearly."

"Beitar is much smaller. Why would Rome even care?"

Simon gave him a cunning grin. "They wouldn't. But now they want me. So they will come for us and we'll be ready."

They reached the encampment where the troops were already packing their gear and getting ready to embark on the trek to the mountainous village. Simon dismounted and, as he did, the boy who had been crying before the attack walked up to him.

"Lord Simon. I'm glad you allowed me to go with the medics. I'm learning a lot. I want to be one of them."

Simon patted his head and said, "Good. Now we're going to Beitar. Are you ready?"

"Yes, but what about the wounded? Some of them can't ride." the boy replied in a concerned tone. Simon knew there was no time to wait for all those soldiers to recover before heading to Beitar. So, he turned to the seemingly concerned boy and said, "We'll take as many as we can in the wagons but some will have to stay here."

The boy solemnly nodded. "I think I'm going to stay here with them, My Lord. They'll need help."

Simon stared at him for a few moment. "What's your name?"

"David." the boy replied.

"A good name. You're a good soldier, David. I'm glad that you want to stay and help the wounded."

In a rather strong reassuring voice, the boy replied. "I'm not afraid, My Lord. Not anymore."

Simon smiled as he patted the boy on the back and walked off.

It was early in the evening, the desert floor was spotted with the Roman's tents. Soldiers had regrouped with their *centuria*. Others tended to their dead and wounded. Clavius turned away from a scout who had just arrived in camp and hurried into the command tent where General Severus was peering at a map of Judea with his commanders. The General was setting out the plan for the next attack. "Once our additional legions arrive, we will surround Ein Gedi and storm the village."

"Excuse me, General. I have some news," Clavius said. "The rebels are abandoning the village."

"They're out in the open?"

"Yes, My Lord."

Severus turned to his commanders. "We must launch an assault now, while there is still time and they are vulnerable."

His commanders were slow to respond. Several hung their heads, looking downtrodden. Clavius understood their dilemma and spoke up for them. "I'm sorry, General, we have too many injuries at this time. We must wait for the rest of the legions before engaging again."

Severus' gaze narrowed and he looked like he was about to shout. But he backed off.

"Fine. Send scouts to follow and see where they are headed."

Clavius motioned for the commanders to leave and they left the tent in haste.

Severus collapsed into a comfortable chair and sighed. "I'm disappointed that we can't attack the rebels now while they are fleeing us. But it's fortunate we have plenty of support on the way. We'll find out where Simon is going and put the full force of our legions against him. He cannot escape us this time."

The exhausted rebel troops and villagers were just arriving on the outskirts of Beitar as the sun was rising and shedding streams of golden light across the terraced, walled village. Located high on a mountainside in the Judean highlands, Beitar was surrounded by towering stone walls -- a veritable fortress.

The hill was covered in boulders of various sizes with vines and shrubbery snaking throughout like tentacles. Narrow pathways wound up the hill to the gates of the city.

Simon had led his caravan of soldiers and citizens slowly up one of such pathways. Tens of thousands of men, women, and children followed along the narrow route bounded by boulders and bushes. It would take all morning before they were all inside the village. Simon felt for a moment as if he were Moses leading the people into the parted Red Sea, away from the Egyptian army that was chasing them.

Simon passed through the gate to the city and walked over to the village square. He had expected a welcoming party, but no residents showed up to greet him. Beitar was an ancient village that had once thrived, but now, less than one hundred people lived here and some of them had joined the rebel force months ago.

Later that day, when thousands had entered the village, he stepped up to a platform in the village square and faced the masses that filled all the streets of the village.

"Within these walls, we will hold Beitar, and she will protect us, and we will stand defiant in the face of Rome! When they come for us, we will be ready."

Uproarious cheers rocked the village and the cheering spread out of the village and down the paths where soldiers and citizens were still arriving through different gates. They were unable to hear what Simon said but were caught up in the response.

"We made it. We made it," Akiva said to his fellow rabbis. However, not everyone seemed pleased with Simon. Rabbis Elazar and Palmer glanced around in disgust, disheartened by the effect the rebel leader had on these people. "Cheer up," Akiva told them. We'll be safer here than where we were." Akiva had ridden most of the way from Ein Gedi in a cart but he'd required help to make it through the steep path to the gate.

"Yes, we're safer here, but for how long?" Palmer said.

Elazar added. "He is quite charismatic, Akiva. I'll give him that. But as I've said before, he is no messiah."

Simon climbed down from the platform and the crowd dispersed. Many were seeking abandoned houses and buildings where they could rest or sleep. Noah, Levi, Rubin, and the rabbis hailed Simon.

"Many years ago, at the time of the first rebellion, rebels built several secret passageways leading to and from the village," Levi said.

"Those could be strategically useful. Make sure they are still functional and assign guards to both ends."

Levi nodded.

"I want these passageways only used by us... and our soldiers," Simon continued and looked among those gathered. Nobody comes in through the tunnels and nobody goes out unless there is a good reason. They all acknowledged what he'd said.

"They need to be inspected for safety," Levi said. "I'll take a look at them."

Rubin laughed. "He knows something about tunnels from our past."

That night, rebel soldiers patrolled the walls, watching the desert for any signs of the Roman legions. Simon checked with the patrols and peered out towards the silvery moonlit landscape. Satisfied that there were no immediate threats from the Romans, he retired to the small house that he, Ruth and Mary had claimed. He walked in to find both of them fast asleep on pads covered with blankets. Ruth woke up as he entered the house.

"Everything all right?" she asked.

He nodded. "For now."

"Wine?"

"Of course."

She poured from a flask into two ceramic cups, then sat down next to him. "It's good to be here with you, Simon, but do you think we can truly hold off the Roman army, My Lord?"

"This fortified village would be a challenge to any army." Simon sipped his wine. "In the end, it won't matter."

Ruth looked alarmed at his comment. "Why do you say that? What do you mean?"

"Every action towards a goal is an end in and of itself. An achievement. The Roman Empire's domination of our country will not die easily, but we are making many cracks in it. One day it will shatter and the Romans will abandon Israel."

"What will happen if we lose this battle?"

"Then our lives will have had a purpose far beyond toiling the fields and feeding our families. We will have left our indelible mark on history itself."

Disturbed by his words, Ruth stood up and turned away.

"Simon, we are still young. We have our whole lives ahead of us. "What of our future? Don't you want a family and a life?"

"I don't know what is in store for us, Ruth."

She turned to face him and raised her voice. "How can you not know? Shouldn't the messiah know such things?"

He noticed Mary moving on her sleeping pad, coming awake. "I am still flesh and blood. I can bleed and die."

"Maybe you should never have put your name on that coin. That only enraged the Roman emperor. I do not wish to die here. I have other desires."

"Such as?"

"To be a mother. I am carrying your child, My Lord."

Simon was taken aback at this unexpected news. He stared off, thinking. "I'm going to have you stay with Rabbi Akiva in a house close to one of the passageways to get you out of Beitar, if necessary."

"What about you? Will you leave this fortress village when the time comes?"

Simon felt torn. Knowing that Ruth was with child tugged at his heart. That distant thought of fleeing Israel for another land, maybe Leon's Greece, came back to haunt him. *No, I could never abandon my country, my army, or my people,* he told himself. "I don't know, Ruth. I really don't."

She nodded, disappointed, and laid back down on her sleeping pad, her back turned to him.

"One more thing."

She rolled over and raised her gaze. "Yes."

"If he's a boy, I want him named Rufus."

She smiled with mixed emotions and closed her eyes.

General Severus and Clavius were listening to one of the captains make comments about the shortage of food for the troops when Clavius was distracted by the sound of the thumping of a galloping horse that was moving in their direction. He moved over to the entrance of the command tent and peered out at the encampment and campfires on the surrounding desert.

A soldier rode swiftly out of the darkness, up to the tent, and dismounted. "Let him in," Clavius told the two guards. Moments later, he and the soldier stepped through the doorway into the lantern glow where Severus had been conferring Clavius and several commanders.

The soldier bowed. "My Lord. The rebels have taken up position in Beitar."

Clavius noticed the confused look on Severus's face and quickly explained. "It's a walled village, General, on a mountain ridge."

"Good. They are cornered. We should attack in the morning."

"More legions will be arriving soon, My Lord," Clavius said. "Maybe it's best to wait to hit them with our full force."

Severus shook his head. The yellow lantern light glazed his features. His eyes narrowed, his frown deepened. "I don't want to delay. We move out at daybreak. We will march on Beitar and take the village quickly. Send messengers and have our incoming legions rendezvous with us there."

Clavius made a slight bow. "Yes, My Lord."

He suspected Severus's decision was more about his own standing with Hadrian than a tactical matter. He wanted full credit for taking down Simon and the rebels. If victory required all of the legions, then his credit would be weakened. But at least he wouldn't have to give up his sword and possibly his life as Marcellus did.

The story of that incident in front of the senate had quickly spread throughout Rome and the military. Hadrian was outraged that Simon had escaped from the Caesarea amphitheater and the general's failure to kill him had cost Marcellus his life. Clavius was sure that the news of both incidents, the outrageous escape and Hadrian's response, had also spread throughout the provinces.

The morning sun was already baking the desert when Severus's legions finally broke camp. The army was so massive that it took nearly an hour before the medics and food wagons at the rear finally started to move. Clavius figured it would take most of the day to reach Beitar. He wasn't looking forward to plotting slowly across the baking desert in the heat of the day. The moderate spring weather had been replaced with the unrelenting daily summer heat. At least, it cooled during the evening and night.

With torch in hand, Levi followed a tunnel inspecting the walls and ceilings for any signs of cracks that could lead to a cave in. He couldn't help thinking about the tunnels that were escape routes in his own village. As a teenager, he had explored the tunnels under Nachum, always avoiding members of the local rebel group who were using the tunnels to store weapons and supplies in hopes of a rebellion against the Romans.

He'd gotten to know the tunnels well and one day, the rebels caught him. That day, he joined the cause and became a tunnel guard. He missed those days when the idea of a rebellion felt like a game, not to be taken too seriously. But all that changed when Simon and his small army arrived at Nachum by boat and somehow drove off the Romans. So, it was natural that he'd volunteered to inspect the tunnels below Beitar. He'd even heard about the tunnels here because the Beitar tunnels were the inspiration for those in Nachum, which were created fifty years earlier.

He was mildly surprised by the size of the tunnels. When he came upon a cavern, he realized there were caves under the hill that had been connected and the passageways between them had expanded. When he came to a second cavern that was illuminated, two guards leaped to their feet and unsheathed their sword. They quickly lowered them when they saw it was one of Simon's generals.

"Has anyone else come through here?" Levi asked, noticing that the pair looked like brothers.

"No sir. Only you," the older of the two replied.

"What are your names?" Levi like to get personal with the soldiers he worked with treating them more like friends than subordinates. It created a greater sense of loyalty as long as they understood his position and respected it.

"I'm Amos and this is my brother, Abraham."

"We're from Hebron," Abraham, the younger one, said.

"Sorry about what happened to your city."

"We'll pay those Romans back for what they did," Amos said.

"That's the spirit. How much farther does this tunnel go?"

"It's just fifty paces or so." Amos pointed to the passage at the far side of the cavern.

"Have you been outside?" Levi inquired.

"We go out every hour and look around."

"But it's warmer in here than outside," Abraham added.

"It is chilly in the mountains at night. But we're at war and could be attacked at any time. I want one of you to be outside on the lookout at all times. You understand?"

"Yes sir," they both responded.

Levi gave them both a stern look, nodded, and moved off. He quickly reached the end of the tunnel where it came out on the hillside. He pushed his way through the thick growth of shrubbery to get a better idea of where the tunnel ended. He'd no sooner stepped out into the open when he glimpsed someone approaching on a galloping horse. He could easily duck back into the shrubbery and the tunnel, but that was not an option for him. He held his ground, one hand on the hilt of his sword. Both guards rushed out with their swords raised.

Levi raised a hand. "Relax, it's one of our scouts."

"Important message for His Majesty, Simon," the scout said and dismounted. He was a short wiry man, an excellent rider, who'd been picked for scouting because of his skills on horseback. But he appeared exhausted and out of breath. He stumbled on a rock and nearly fell over.

"Follow me." Levi, with torch in hand, led the scout and his horse through the dark tunnel and towards the village. He wanted to ask the scout about his message but Simon had ordered scouts to only talk to him. Levi guessed the reason was that Simon was convinced there was a spy among them. A scout's message might never get to Simon if the wrong person intercepted it. Because of that concern, Levi didn't bother asking the scout any personal questions, as he'd done with the guards. The message was too important and they needed to find Simon as quickly as possible.

Chapter 20

Simon was discussing the best ways of defending the village with Noah, Rubin, the commanders, and the rabbis when Levi walked into the command center, a wood frame building adjacent to the village square. With him was the scout.

"We have news," Levi said, and everyone turned to him and the scout.

"What is it?" Simon asked, seemingly annoyed by the interruption.

"The Romans will be here by nightfall," the scout said.

"Are you certain about that?"

"Yes, My Lord."

Simon turned his attention back to the assembled group. "We can hold them off for some time here. Possibly forever. "

Rabbi Elazar scoffed. "No, that's impossible. It doesn't matter that the village is fortified. Our food, water and weaponry will be depleted in months, or weeks even."

Simon glanced at Noah.

"True, My Lord."

"Dispatch a hundred men to the nearest town to bring back as much food and water and other supplies as they can carry."

Noah nodded and was about to leave when Levi stepped forward. "I'll lead it, My Lord."

"Very well. But don't waste any time making friends."

Everyone laughed in spite of the seriousness of the matter. "Of course not."

Levi hurried out of the command center. Within seconds, everyone in the room could hear him shouting for soldiers.

"With the Roman assault imminent, we need to position the troops immediately on full alert. We'll need to place them in the best possible positions. The archers all along the walls, of course. I want all the smiths to work non-stop creating arrows for them. They should tear down any non-essential structure for the raw materials."

"What about sending some troops outside the village to slow down their attack?" Rubin asked.

"That's insane. That's suicide," Rabbi Palmer snapped. "They'll be slaughtered for no good reason."

"He's right," Simon said, grudgingly. "If they retreat, the Romans will follow their path to the village."

Within minutes, the village was a hive of activity with soldiers readying their weapons for combat. A group of young soldiers gathered around Simon as he demonstrated the best techniques for sharpening their swords on grindstones. He moved on and watched the smiths working diligently to create arrows.

"Some of these aren't the straightest arrow ever," he said holding one up. But they'll do when the archers are aiming at large numbers of troops. He walked up on the wall where archers were already finding their stations, testing their bows, and preparing for the battle.

Levi rode through the tunnel he'd inspected earlier with dozens of soldiers following. They dismounted and walked their horses through the shrouded mouth of the passageway. Several soldiers had attached carts to their horses for carrying water back and the carts shredded the shrubbery. Once they'd all emerged, they rode off heading in the opposite direction from the Romans. The nearest village was about an hour away and they would have to gather as much food as possible as quickly as possible and get back to the village before the Romans arrived.

Soon after they reached the village, Levi realized they weren't going to get much help there. Like Beitar, very few people lived here and they begged Levi not to take away their only food. An old man told them that some of the villagers had joined the rebels and others had fled to a village two hours away by horse on the west side of the Dead Sea. "You will find food and water there."

Ruth and Mary sat at the table in their house talking about the past; playing in the streets of Jerusalem, going to the market with their mothers, and taking an interest in boys. It was a way for Ruth to avoid thinking about their situation. At least in Ein Gedi, she'd felt that she had a good life for months, nearly a year. Here, she felt they were hiding and waiting, and she didn't want to think what the end result would be for her there, for Simon, Mary, and the thousands of others.

Whether it's today, tomorrow, next week or next month, she knew the Romans would find them here. She was terrified by the idea of thousands of enemy soldiers surrounding them and assaulting the village until they breached the walls. She couldn't help but think about the story of Masada and the faith of its people sixty years ago as they also were in a fortified village surrounded by thousands of the Roman soldiers. But she'd made the choice to spend her life with Simon no matter what was in store.

Now she was with child and where would the child be born? Where would they live? Could any offspring of Simon live in peace or would the Romans come after him or her? Bringing a child into this world – especially Simon's child - was a terrible dilemma.

"What are you thinking about, Ruth?" Mary said when Ruth had stopped talking and gazed off.

"Listen, something's going on outside." She heard the sound of pounding footsteps passing their door and distant shouts.

They got up, walked over to the door and stepped outside. Soldiers rushed about, and a captain shouted orders. The house was adjacent to the village square. They'd no sooner closed the door behind them when Rabbi Akiva walked over to them. "It's best if you two stay in your house. It's too dangerous now. Especially in your condition, Ruth."

"Rabbi Akiva, what's going on?"

"The Romans are coming soon."

Mary took her arm. "We better do what he says."

"Is there anything we can do to help?" Ruth asked.

"You've already been a big help, Ruth. You helped save Simon in Caesarea. But now you're with child and should be resting. Leave the fighting to the soldiers."

They retreated inside and sat back down. Ruth shook her head. "If the Romans get into the village, then no place is safe."

"Don't think about it that way, Ruth. We're protected. The village is a fortress."

"I know, but it doesn't feel that way right now. It's frustrating that we can't do anything."

"It's not our place, until they need our help. So we need to be ready."

Ruth considered her comment and wanted to believe that they could assist in some way and wouldn't be shunned. "And how did that Akiva know about my condition?"

Mary looked at her, smiled. "Your condition is getting quite visible. Word spreads because of who you are."

"Yes, and I wish we were married. But Simon hesitates still."

Moments later, Simon entered the house and sighed. He was clearly troubled. This was a side of him Ruth had never seen before. Always, even in the worst of situations, Simon had always seen it somehow as an advantage.

"Are you okay, Simon?

"The Romans are coming."

"We heard."

He looked at her with longing. She got up and hugged him. He placed a gentle hand on her stomach. "I'm sorry I brought you here."

"I'm fine, Simon. I want to be by your side, wherever it takes us." She cupped his face in her hands. "Just make it back to me. I want our child to have a father."

He solemnly nodded. "I will. I promise. And I'll make you my wife." They held each other tightly. Mary smiled and looked away.

◦◦◦

Sabrina was laying on her side of the luxurious bed in a nightgown when Hadrian walked in clutching a note. She could tell immediately that he was in a sour mood. "What is it now, Hadrian?"

"Our spy within the rebels has informed us that Simon's woman is pregnant." He crumpled the note and dropped it on the floor.

She sat up in bed and looked perplexed. "I don't understand. Why is this troubling? It has nothing to do with the rebellion."

He walked up to her and glared. "You should know why," he snapped and backhanded her across the face. She crumpled to her side and placed a hand on her flushed cheek. She stared up at him in shock and fear. He stormed out of the room and she began weeping, her tears flowed as she despaired. He blamed her but she was sure it was his fault they were childless.

◦◦◦

Simon moved among the archers on the walls, who gripped their bows and quivers and offered words of encouragement. "Wait until the Romans are well within your range, then fire your arrows as quickly as you can. Others will feed you more arrows. We have thousands of them ready for you."

Rubin walked up to him. "All archers are in place, my Lord."

"Good. The Romans will taste our arrowheads if they dare come too close."

Rubin stepped closer and lowered his voice. "My Lord, there is much concern among the troops that this effort is suicide, and that we can't stop them. That we are facing the end. We need a rabbi, a spiritual figure, to boost morale among the soldiers."

Simon agreed with a nod. "Send for a rabbi. Any will do, except for Akiva. I already have him on a special assignment."

"Thank you, sir." Rubin walked away.

After Simon had left the house, a wave of sadness washed over Ruth and she felt like she was drowning in despair. Mary tried to comfort her but nothing she said had any effect. Finally, Ruth stood up and wiped the tears from her cheeks. "Let's go!"

"What, go where?"

"Out. Let's go see what's going on. I don't care what the rabbi said."

They left the house and walked over to the nearby village square where rabbis and others who weren't in the rebel army were gathered. Some were openly weeping, others looked frightened. One woman shouted: "*HaShem* take us now. Before the Romans get us!" The rabbis tried to console the woman and others who were equally distraught.

Ruth couldn't see much from where she stood but she felt an intense pressure as if something massive was moving their way and she knew it would destroy the village and everyone in it.

"I don't like it here much," Mary said, holding Ruth's hand. "These people all think we're going to die. Did you hear that woman calling for God to take us now?"

Akiva walked over to them. "You see, Ruth, it's better to stay inside. You don't need to hear the wails of these people. There's nothing you can do for them."

She nodded and was about to leave when a soldier rushed up to the rabbis. "Prince Simon needs a rabbi up on the wall right away for spiritual guidance. Many are so fearful."

"So he's a messiah and a prince," Elazar muttered.

Akiva ignored the comment. "I would do it but Simon wants me to stay close to Ruth."

"I'll do it," Elazar said.

"May God be with you."

Ruth gave Elazar a warm hug, then he headed for the wall with the soldier.

"I'm surprised that you are so kind to him," Akiva said. "He is such a critic of Simon, you know."

"Unfortunately, I'm beginning to believe what Elazar said," Ruth commented as she watched the slight rabbi move out of sight.

"Which is?" Akiva asked.

"That this is suicide."

"Our messiah has led us to victory thus far."

His words didn't ease her fear. She placed a hand on her belly and wondered if she would live to see her child born.

Clavius rode up to General Severus as the enormous Roman army moved towards Beitar. "We just received word, General, that additional legions are arriving as we speak.

Severus momentarily looked disappointed. "Excellent, I guess. But I'm not so sure we will even need them."

When Clavius didn't respond, he asked if something was disturbing him. "What is it, Clavius?"

"I've been told our troops are becoming battle-weary and are fearful that the fortified village will be difficult to take without massive casualties."

Severus glared daggers at him. "We are Romans! We cannot be defeated. Have the legions surround Beitar as soon as we get there. Make sure that the ones on the inside, closest to the fortified village, have shields. The rebels will certainly send their arrows at the troops."

"Yes, My Lord. He rode off to pass the message to the commanders.

"They're here!" one of the archers hollered.

"They're coming, my Lord!" a captain shouted.

Soldiers crowded the wall and when they glimpsed at the overwhelming size of the army and saw that more troops were coming from as far as they could see, fear reverberated throughout those gathered.

"Everyone maintain your positions," Simon said, firmly, sounding confident. He knew that if even a hint of fear was noticed in his voice, it would only make matters worse. If the troops panicked, they would be quickly overrun. "We will commence with my plan." He turned and strode away.

Chapter 21

In the valley below Beitar, a sea of shields and swords surrounded the village. Tents were erected, and the Roman army was settling in. Severus stood in front of the command tent staring up at Beitar in anticipation. The rebels had no chance. He was confident the village would fall at his command. The additional legions would be here only for show, to invoke fear. They wouldn't be needed.

Clavius promptly rode up. "General, each of the four walls surrounding the city has but a single gate. Our battalions are prepared to charge the gates and breach the village on your command.

No sense wasting any time, Severus thought. The quicker the rebel army collapsed, the more credit he would receive from Rome. "Very well. Commence with the assault immediately."

Clavius grinned with pleasure and rode off.

Rubin marched along the wall, passing archers standing ready. Captains farther down the line shouted: "They're attacking!"

Rubin peered over the wall and saw the Roman soldiers storming up the pathway towards the gate on the side where he stood. Cries from along the wall told him that they were attacking the other three side of the village as well.

"Archers commence!" Rubin bellowed. The order traveled down the line, along the wall repeated by one captain after another. Archers released their arrows, arcing them skyward and they rained down on the Romans, some were stopped by shields, others found their mark. But their effort did nothing to stop the Romans, who scrambled up the mountainside paths. It wasn't long before the initial surge of soldiers came too close to the wall for the arrows to be effective. But more soldiers were arriving so the archers continued filling the sky with arrows.

Rubin knew that all four gates were about to be breached.

Simon was ready for them. As the Romans climbed towards the main gate, he and dozens of rebel soldiers emerged from behind boulders and surprised the exhausted Romans. Simon swiftly hacked down several soldiers. As soon as more approached along the narrow path, they were met by rebel blades. Swords clashed and clanged and one after another, the Romans fell to the rebel swords. Simon knew the rebels at the other three gates were doing the same. He was confident they were holding firm and Roman blood was flowing down the mountainside.

Shocked Romans stumbled over the corpses of fallen comrades, and before long, the bodies were blocking the approach to the gates. The Romans near the top turned and pushed against the tide of troops, creating confusion and chaos. Word spread among the close-packed Roman troops that it was a trap. They turned en masse and retreated. As they did so, they were greeted with arrows striking their backs and dropping many of them.

Rebels on the wall and on the ground cheered their victory. Once again, Simon had tricked the Roman army and far fewer troops had repelled the Rome's legions.

Clavius entered the command tent, where Severus stood stone-faced in the aftermath of the bloodbath. "We couldn't overpower them. The bodies of our troops piled up and blocked our advance."

"Those were soldiers, good soldiers, you're talking about, Clavius. They weren't logs blocking your way."

"It's Simon again. He did the same sort of thing to Marcellus in the narrow valley by the Dead Sea."

"You don't have to remind me. Unlike Marcellus, we are not going to withdraw. We will stay here until every one of those rebels is dead. Including Simon." He lifted his head. "Listen to them, cheering and celebrating as if they won."

"They won't be cheering for long." Clavius tried to reassure the general. But he had no idea how they were going to conquer the fortified village.

"This will require more than brute force and numbers," Severus said.

The rebels celebrated their victory in the town square with soldiers taking turns talking about how the battle went at their gate. A cheer went up after each story of the Romans being beaten back and retreating. Hundreds of dead Roman bodies now blocked the gates to the village and the Romans would have to clear them away and face more arrows from the archers.

Abruptly, Simon rode up into the square on horseback scattering people in his path. "Cease! No celebrating. This is no time for festivities!" The crowd fell silent except for a few mutters. Simon continued: "We have defeated the Romans on their first attempt but we have much work ahead of us. Has Levi and his men returned with food and water?"

Rubin stepped up. "No, My Lord. They have not."

"What is the status of our provisions?"

"It is depleting at a more rapid rate than we projected," Rubin responded. "Probably no more than a few weeks remain."

"We will begin rationing it immediately. One third portions for all."

The crowd groaned and began dispersing. Simon knew that he had disappointed those that gathered. He was aware that his appearance at gatherings usually provided people with a reason to feel confident and reassured, and a sense that a higher power, the messiah, was present among them. But now they were not only disappointed that he had taken away their momentary feelings of joy from their victory, but instead of magically providing them with an abundance of food, he was depriving them.

Early the next morning, Rabbi Elazar moved with purposeful haste down the street until he reached the hidden entrance of a tunnel, a secret passageway in and out of the village. He looked around, making sure that no one noticed him lingering there. Then he slipped inside. He moved through the dark passage without a torch, feeling his way along the walls. He was relieved when he noticed a faint illumination in the distance. He moved ahead with purpose and was ready when he saw the torch and two guards near the opening leading out of the passageway.

"What is your business, rabbi?"

"Our men haven't yet returned with food and water. I want to pray for their safe return. Since they are outside the village, I want to show our resolve to God by praying for them."

"You should do it here," one of the guards said. "It's dangerous outside the village. Only guards are supposed to go out there."

Elazar scrutinized the pair and guessed they were brothers. "What village are you two from?" They told him and he turned to the older of the two. "If you had never left the safety of Gophna, you would not be here with the messiah defending your country."

The two men stared at him and he realized that they probably wished they were back in their village. He took a different approach. "I am a rabbi and I have a higher calling. I need to pray outside the village because Levi and the soldiers with the supplies are also outside."

That seemed to work but the older of the two said he would go with him and stand guard. Elazar smiled. "I have God to protect me. I will be fine and be back in a few minutes."

The guard hesitated, then nodded, and Elazar quickly moved towards the passage leading to the mouth of the passageway. Once outside, he disappeared down the slope and into a wooded area.

The sun was rising over the desert as Simon looked out at the endless Roman camps spread across the landscape. Guards stood watch every ten paces along the entire wall ready to call out the moment the Romans showed any sign of preparing for another attack. But if Levi never returned with the food, the enemy could simply wait and starve the rebel army into submission, Simon thought. But the Romans didn't know they were short of food, he reminded himself. That was an advantage they had. Besides, he knew they wanted him. The capture or killing of Simon, Son of Star, would be their greatest prize along with the destruction of the rebel army. But the Roman general probably worried that the longer they waited, the more chance that Simon would slip away.

A soldier approached and called out to him. "May I have a word with you, My Lord?"

"What is it, soldier?"

"It's about Rabbi Elazar."

"Go on."

"I was watching the entrance to one of the passageways as I was assigned. The rabbi didn't see me standing out of sight in the doorway of a building."

"Get on with it. What did he do?"

"He looked around as if he didn't want to be seen. Then he went into the passageway?"

"Thank you for that. Now return to your position and let me know if you see him return."

Severus paced about the command tent as Clavius and the top commanders awaited the next directive in the war effort. "They've demonstrated their advantage on the high ground, but we have them surrounded, which is to our advantage," the general began.

"They will eventually run out of resources," Clavius said. "They have no new source of food."

"But when?"

"They might last a few weeks by limiting the rations."

"A few weeks? I don't want to wait that long. We've got to catch Simon off-guard."

"I've got an idea," Clavius said. "Their supply of water is outside the village. As a gesture of goodwill, we could allow them access to it. But we poison the well."

Severus shook his head. "First, that's also our main source of water and besides, they would never believe any kind of goodwill gesture on our part."

Severus looked up to see a soldier standing at the entrance to the tent. "What is it?"

"Sorry to interrupt, general, but I have a report on the enemy."

Levi and his troops slowly traversed the wooded area on their horses, carrying saddlebags of food and pulling carts with containers of water. The second village they had entered had food and water in abundance but the village governor insisted that his leadership counsel meet the next morning and decide what and how much to provide. When Levi had asked if they could meet immediately, the governor said the morning was the earliest they could act. Levi could tell that if he argued, they might be sent on their way with nothing. Once approved, it took more hours to negotiate and gather the goods.

Now they were getting near Beitar and could smell the campfires from the Roman encampment. The plan was to rest until the middle of the night, then charge through a weak point in the Roman encampment and slip into one of the secret passageways.

Levi silently signaled his men to stop. No one moved as the soldiers waited for orders. It seemed like a good place to rest and wait with large rocks sheltering them. But he sensed that something wasn't right about this place. That's when he heard the crunch of leaves from somewhere nearby. Suddenly, from all sides, the Romans emerged from behind the rocks, trees and bushes.

Levi realized they were hopelessly trapped and outnumbered as more Romans crowded around them.

Simon and several soldiers were tearing down a wood building and using their swords to virtually slice pieces of wood into thin strips that they tossed onto a pile. Ruth and Mary scooped up the wood pieces and carried them over to the smiths who were turning out arrows for the archers. On one side of the smiths were the wood strips and on the other side were a large pile of metal arrowheads that the smiths had been accruing over the past three years.

Simon wasn't surprised that Ruth was eager to help. He wanted the two women to stay out of the way and preferably in the house, but they had come out and watched him demolish the building. After Ruth realized the strips of wood in the pile were for the smiths, she and Mary volunteered to deliver the pieces. He knew there was no point in arguing with her so he quickly agreed.

He looked up as Rubin hurried over to him. "Simon! Come to the wall! Hurry!"

Simon, Rubin and others rushed up the ladders to the wall. Once there, Rubin jammed a finger towards the Roman troops just outside the archers' range. Levi was in front of the troops seated on a horse, his chest and arms bound by ropes. The same Roman general who had tried to feed him to the lion in Caesarea stood next to him.

"Simon, Son of Star, I think you remember me. You got away from the lion but you're not going to escape me and all the legions who are coming for you. Not this time. We know you are almost out of food and water. Surrender now and you and your people will live. If not, you condemn yourself and the others to death."

Simon blinked at this unexpected and tragic turn of events. He glanced around at his men, looking to him for guidance. He looked down off the wall to Ruth. She nodded to him no doubt hoping that he'll accept the offer. He wasn't certain what to do until he heard a shout from Levi.

"Simon. Don't do it, My Lord."

His features hardened with resolve as he looked down upon Severus. "Leave Israel, General, and I'll let you and your men live."

Severus nodded to a soldier, who brandished a sword and quickly decapitated Levi. His head tumbled away as his body went limp and slid off the horse.

"You have sealed your fate today, Simon," Severus called out.

"The only fate sealed this day is Rome's," he answered.

Severus and his men moved off. Simon passively turned away.

Chapter 22

Simon, Rubin, Noah and several of the rebel captains were standing in the command center building silent and sullen. They were expecting Rabbi Elazar to join them. When he finally arrived, they glared at him.

"You summoned me, Simon?"

"Yes. You were seen leaving the village through a secret passageway."

"Yes, I was going out to pray for Levi and his men."

Simon approached him in a threatening manner. "Seems your prayers did no good."

Elazar looked nervous as Simon loomed over him. "We can pray but none of us know God's will."

"Perhaps you didn't pray. Perhaps you informed the Romans of our situation." Simon shouted at the rabbi, his voice reflecting his rising anger. "By collaborating with the enemy, you have risked our Divine protection."

"I did no such thing," he stammered. "I prayed...prayed for their safe return."

"Liar!" Simon snapped and savagely hit him in the jaw, sending the frail rabbi into the wall, where he crumpled in a heap.

Noah went over to him, then stood and solemnly faced Simon. "He's dead."

Simon simply nodded. Some of the captains appeared shocked that Simon had killed a rabbi.

Rabbi Akiva was leading several rabbis in prayer in the village square hoping the Divine power would help save the rebels. A captain approached him, interrupted the prayer and whispered in Akiva's ear. The rabbi's eyes widened and his jaw dropped. The captain walked away and Akiva faced the rabbis.

"What is it, Akiva?" Palmer called out. "Please tell us what disturbs you."

Akiva nodded solemnly. "If Simon killed Rabbi Elazar, as I've been told, then he is not our messiah. The messiah will never break any of the Ten Commandments. We have no messiah. God have mercy on us."

A desperate angry crowd of mostly civilians – citizens of Beitar or families from Ein Gedi - was gathered in the village square. Shouts of despair arose when they saw Simon approaching. "We are thirsty! We are hungry!"

Simon mounted a platform, looked over the crowd and commanded: "Silence!"

"But we are almost out of food and water," a woman called out to him. What are we going to do?"

"I said silence!"

The crowd quiets to low grumbling. A man stepped forward, a resident of Beitar. "We should surrender, My Lord! Rome will spare us!"

The crowd mumbled in agreement.

"Lies! All lies!" Simon shouted. "Surrender is not an option."

The crowd disagreed and several people shouted at Simon in protest.

"Even if that were true, and Rome did not put you all to the sword, do you want to return to the Roman subservience?"

The crowd erupted, some agreeing, many resisting. "Better than dying!" someone shouted.

"Or starving!" someone else yelled from the back of the crowd.

"Silence!"

The crowd quieted down again. Simon dropped his chin, thinking... and formed a plan. After a few moments, he raised his gaze and explained: "I want all our women to gather clothes requiring cleaning. I want them to use one-fourth of our water to wash those clothes."

The crowd erupted in protest again. "Our water…. We need our water."

"Quiet! Now!" Simon responded.

The shouts died down. "And I want the clothes hung to dry along the top of the outside walls, so the Romans can see them.

Most of the crowd stared blankly at Simon, but many looked at Simon as if he's lost his mind.

"Go! Do it now!"

The crowd dispersed, but they didn't go quietly. The muttering, shaking of heads, and disconsolate comments continued.

The sun was just peeking over the desert horizon and Severus was enjoying his breakfast when Clavius hurried into the command tent.

"General, you must see this. Look what the rebels are doing."

Severus furrowed his brow, threw his napkin down, and stood up. "Now what's that Simon doing?"

They strode out of the tent and looked up the cliff at the village. Rebel laundry blew in the wind all along the walls. Severus shook his head in annoyance. "There has been no rain in weeks. Where have they gotten this water supply?"

"Our rebel spy said they were out of water. He must have been lying."

"If he shows up again with information, kill him."

Clavius nodded. "What are we going to do, continue to wait them out?"

"Send a messenger to Rome with the following: *Your Highness, the rebels have a large supply of water and probably food.*

Simon was about to enter his house and wondered if Ruth had heard about Elazar. He knew she was sympathetic towards the rabbi even though Elazar was critical of him. "Simon, stop. I want to talk to you."

He turned to see Akiva approaching, and he knew instantly what it was about. "I didn't kill him intentionally. But I did kill him. And he might be responsible for killing the rest of us."

"What do you mean by that?"

Simon told him about the soldier who had spotted Elazar.

"Just because he went into the passageway doesn't prove he left the village and talked to the Romans."

"Two guards at the end of the passageway let him go out to pray. When he came back in from his praying, one of the guards went outside and saw several Romans looking up towards entrance and pointing."

"Elazar shouldn't have gone outside to pray. That was a mistake. But it was no reason to kill him. Did you kill the guard who also gave away the location of the entrance?"

"Akiva, it wasn't just about revealing the location of the entrance. It was worse than that. One of the Romans called up to the guard and shouted, "No more food and water for you, and you know what happens after that."

Akiva nodded solemnly, thinking over what he'd heard. "Yes, no more food and water."

As they talked, Simon had noticed the bright sunlight had vanished and the day had turned a sullen gray. At that moment, the wind picked up and swirled around them in the alleyway where they stood. The sky lit up as lightning flashed and was followed moments later by a sharp crack of thunder. They both looked up in surprise and abruptly were pelted by a deluge of rain. Stunned, they turned palms and faces to the sky. No rain, not even a drizzle, had fallen in at least a couple of months.

Akiva dropped to his knees. "God has answered our prayers. Let us give thanks, Simon. Pray with me."

But Simon's mind was elsewhere. Without another word, he raced off, leaving Akiva on his knees, as the storm intensified and the rain drenched the village. Soldiers and civilians were filling the streets shouting for joy but Simon knew it was no time to pray or cheer.

He grabbed two soldiers by the arms. "Open the cisterns! Hurry!" He rushed over to other soldiers and told them the same. The covers of the cisterns were in place to save water from evaporating and now they needed to remove them as quickly as possible.

As the storm continued unabated, dirty water rolled in waves down the side of the mountain, quickly flooding the Roman encampment. The wind knocked over tents and soldiers slogged through knee-deep water. Even the command tent located at the highest point in the valley was awash with rainwater.

Clavius clambered through the raging storm and rushed into the command tent. Severus stood in ankle-deep water, looking miserable as the storm raged on. "What did you find out?" Severus asked.

"Our food supply is safe for now. Lots of tents have been blown away. Soldiers are dealing with the storm as best they can."

"What about attacking right now? The rebels would be caught off guard."

Clavius's eyes widened. "General, it would be impossible to get to the gates. Plus the soldiers are in disarray in no condition to attack during the storm."

"This is war and wars are not always fought in good weather."

Severus was in a bad mood and Clavius knew he was going to persist. He needed some way to assuage him. "I will get a couple of soldiers and we will attempt to approach the village."

Clavius slogged the entry to the tent where the cover flaps were whipping in the wind. He stepped outside and surveyed the chaotic scene. Sodden soldiers were struggling to upright their tents. Others just stood in the rain, some staring towards the river of water flowing down the mountain. Severus stepped next to him. "Don't just attempt to approach the village, Clavius. Do it."

He pointed to a pair of soldiers who stood together with their backs to the wind. "Take those two. They're not doing anything."

"Yes, sir."

He approached the soldiers. Both were young and wiry, probably from the same village and related. He ordered them to follow him. "We're in a storm, sir," the taller of the two said. "Where are we going?"

"Up to the village gate."

They both looked puzzled. "You can't be serious, sir."

"I am. Let's go."

Reluctantly, they followed him. The wind was starting to abate and the rain was lighter by the time they reached the base of the nearest trail leading to the village. But water still flowed down the mountain in a heavy torrent and threatened to knock them over if they started climbing.

Clavius was uncertain what to do until an arrow struck the shoulder of one of the soldiers. Suddenly, more arrows pierced the ground around them and they ran through the water back to the camp. Clavius felt an arrow graze his shoulder, then another struck his helmet. But the two soldiers had no such luck. Both collapsed with arrows protruding from their backs. So much for climbing to the village, Clavius thought, and dragged the bodies through the water back to the camp. More arrows flew past them.

Hadrian leaned forward on his plush throne, his shoulders tense, and his jaw jutting forward defiantly. He could hardly read the letter because his hands were shaking in anger.

It may take months, if not longer, for their supply to run dry.

He crushed the letter in his fist, stood up and faced the commanders who had brought the letter to the palace. Enraged, he stared hard at them. I want all the legions in Arabia to go immediately to Beitar. That includes Gallica, Ferrata, Cyrenaica, and Fretensis. I want them to attack those walls with every sword we have, with every spear we have -- to the last one!"

One of the generals stepped forward. "Your Majesty, we are already spread so thin in Arabia and we are having difficulty controlling uprisings. The Judea rebels have awakened all of Arabia. If those legions go to Beitar, it will endanger the lives of our civilian administrators. Even now, they are in grave danger when traveling without military support."

"All the more reason to crush this Son of Star. I don't care if it takes all the Roman military to destroy that rebellion. Now go! All of you."

The commanders rush out of the room.

Two weeks after the life-saving rainstorm passed, Simon stood on the wall with rebel troops and knew that the days of waiting were over. They'd watched more legions arrive and surround the village. They were so numerous that it seemed as if every soldier in the Roman army had been sent to Beitar to capture the village and decimate the rebel force.

Captains shouted orders directing soldiers to stand at attention and raise their swords as they faced the village. It was a show of strength, an attempt to frighten the rebels into submission, Simon thought as he stared at the formation of the assembled Romans. He was calm, accepting whatever fate awaited him.

After a couple of hours, the soldiers retreated and set up an even larger encampment than the one they had looked out on for weeks. Tomorrow, or the day after that, they would be back to assault the village. This many soldiers would not remain long as passive observers. They were here to wage war.

So it has begun, he thought.

That night, a huge bonfire burned in the center of the village square, where soldiers and civilians were gathered and spilling out into the surrounding streets. Simon stepped up onto a platform and raised a hand to call everyone's attention. "Tomorrow, the ninth day of the lunar month Av, is the fast of Tisha B'Av, and the day of our reckoning. On the eve of this battle, we rise and fight as free men. We have brought the undefeated Roman Empire and its mighty army to their knees. We have freed our land for three years now."

He raised a silver coin, the firelight glistened and danced on it. "We have stamped our story on this precious metal. So, no matter the outcome tomorrow, we have made history. It will be written on the pages of time for future generations to see! For thousands of years to come!"

Simon raised his clenched fists and gritted his teeth. "It is better to die a free man than to live as a slave!"

The crowd cheered with many raising fists, others raising their swords. Simon climbed down from the platform and walked over to Rubin. "You are not to participate in the battle tomorrow, Rubin. Do you understand?"

He looked perplexed. "Why not, My Lord?"

"I have another assignment for you."

Ruth laid awake in bed, now large with pregnancy. Simon entered the house, took off his armor and settled on the bed next to her. He puts his hand on her belly.

"It ends tomorrow. No matter what happens, I'll be with you."

She puts her face against his chest and they held each other. She tried her best not to cry but the tears rolled down her cheeks and onto Simon. "I don't want you to die. I want to live on with you and our child."

"If it is meant to be, it will be."

Early the next morning, Clavius trotted his horse in front of endless rows of Roman soldiers. He circled the entire village, then approached Severus who was standing in front of the command tent.

"I have inspected all the troops who are prepared to attack, General. Our men are ready."

"Very good. We shall…"

Severus was interrupted by someone calling to him. "General, look!"

He turned to see a commander pointing up at the village. Severus and Clavius looked up and couldn't believe what they saw. Beitar's main gate was open. They stared in confusion, and moments later, a commander rode up and reported that another gate was open. In short order, they learned all four gates were open as if the rebels were welcoming the Romans.

"General, what do you think it means? Do you think they want to surrender?" Clavius asked.

Severus shook his head. "No, it's another trick by Simon. But it doesn't matter. Commence the attack immediately. There will be no retreat under any circumstance. We will overwhelm them. No matter how long it takes."

Clavius galloped away, shouting: "Storm the fortress now! Storm Beitar now!"

Simon watched the action from the wall almost as if he were observing it from afar and not a participant. Battle cries filled the air as waves of Roman soldiers closed in on the village. Archers on the walls rained death on the encroaching army. But they kept coming and clamored over their own dead, mounting the rocky terrain on either side of the paths.

More arrows showered down. So many that they blotted out the sun. But the Romans continued their slow stampede towards the village. The open maws of the gates filled with rebel soldiers waiting for the inevitable hand-to-hand combat. Simon took his position beside Noah. Their swords were drawn as they watched the Romans approach, pressing on against the continued onslaught of arrows.

Simon raised his sword. "It is time. It's a good day to die! For Israel!"

He charged forward, Noah on his heels and thousands of rebel soldiers behind them. He knew rebels were flowing out of all the gates and collided with the oncoming Romans. Sunlight sparkled off the slashing blades as swords clanged against one another, and soldiers were felled on both sides.

Simon and Noah fought side by side, dropping one Roman after another. Their blades were slick with blood which also was splattered across their faces and over their fighting apparel. Near the gates, on the paths and in the valley, the Roman and rebel bodies piled up. But both sides continued fighting.

Simon hacked, slashed and thrusted as if he was possessed with boundless energy. Fallen Romans lined the path along his movement away from the gate. He spun and danced across the battlefield, swinging his deadly sharp and shiny metal blade before him. Time seemed to move in slow motion, and for a few moments, it felt as if he was watching himself from outside his body as he took on another Roman warrior. Then, the action completely froze and he glimpsed at a smiling, nodding image of Master Leon. They locked gazes for a moment, reaffirming their sacred connection. Instantly, the action resumed as Simon blocked a sword, then slashed the soldier's throat.

He spun about only to see Noah being hacked to death. *Godspeed, my friend. You served Israel and me well.* Simon continued on, a one-man death machine. But it was futile. The Romans breached the city, passing through the gates, killing everyone they crossed, be it man, woman, or child. The rebel soldiers fought valiantly but were hopelessly outnumbered.

Chapter 23

ON THE MORNING AFTER THE battle, death permeated the air and blood saturated the ground as General Severus began his tour of the battlefield. He scanned the scene in front of him from the valley to the nearest path up to the village. Dead Romans were piled as far as the eye could see. The sight of so many corpses of his soldiers was almost too dreadful to bear.

He slipped on the blood-soaked path and dropped to his hands and knees next to the bloodied remains of a teenage soldier. The boy's jaw had been sheared off by a blade. His eye stared sightlessly skyward. The smell of death closed in around him; Severus gagged and vomited his breakfast. A couple members of his entourage helped him to his feet. He was shaken, despondent. Never before in his years in the Roman military had he seen so much death. Now, he knew what a hollow victory felt like.

"Would you like to return to the camp, sir?" his adjutant asked.

"No, I want to get to the village."

"It's worse, sir, as we go higher."

"I know. I need to see it."

"We beat them, sir, beat them good,"

"Yes... but at what cost?"

Captains and commanders and other soldiers walked among the corpses surveying the carnage and searching for survivors. Severus stopped and caught his breath as he saw Clavius, his body peppered with arrows. He dropped to one knee, reached for Clavius's shoulder, shook it and uttered his name.

"He's dead, sir. I'm sorry," the adjunct said.

"General!" a commander called out from where several soldiers gazed at a corpse. Disconsolate, he walked over and gazed at a corpse.

"This one has been identified as Simon, Son of Star," the commander said.

Simon lay on his back, staring blankly, surrounded by Roman corpses. He was covered in wounds, some surprisingly deep. "With those wounds, how could he have kept fighting like that?" Severus uttered. In death, he still clutched his sword.

The sun glinted off something around his neck. The general leaned a bit closer, squinted. It was a necklace with a coin hanging from it. Severus ripped it from Simon's neck and looked at the over-stamped Roman coin bearing Simon's name. Enraged, the general hurled the coin away. "Carry him to our camp. We will take him with us to Rome as proof for Hadrian to see."

Rubin clutched a torch as he led Ruth and Mary and the rabbis through a darkened tunnel, the longest of the hidden passages that took them far from the village.

"How much farther?" complained Palmer.

"Almost there, Rabbi."

After another half an hour of walking, they emerged from the mouth of the tunnel into bright sunlight and walked their way through the thick underbrush that hid the entrance.

Rebel soldiers on horseback waited in a clearing with extra horses. One of them walked over to Rubin. "How many more are still coming, General?" he asked.

Rubin shook his head. "There are no others."

"They're all dead," Palmer said. "The fool led us to our destruction."

No one had the strength or will to protest. Not even Ruth, who was heavy with Simon's child. Palmer took their silence as a sign they agreed with him.

"Simon bar...Koziba!" he said, mockingly. "That's who he is from this day on."

"Koziba? What does that mean?" Rubin asked.

Rabbi Akiva answered. "It means son of the lie."

Rubin turned to Palmer. "Watch what you say about Simon. He did more for Israel's freedom from the Romans than all the rest of us together!"

"And look where it has gotten us," Palmer snapped. "Death and destruction."

Everyone exchanged glances and Rubin sensed that some of them agreed with Palmer. He turned to Ruth. "Just ignore him." She looked too exhausted to even reply.

He handed her a note. "Simon told me to give this to you when it was all over."

She nodded sadly and opened it. It read:

My love. Our future together was always uncertain. Though I moved forth with utmost confidence, I always had doubts. Please know it was you who gave me the strength and courage to see this through to the end. You calmed my soul through all of it. I hope you live a long and peaceful life of freedom with our child, whether I'm by your side or not. In my heart we are husband and wife. And have been since the moment our eyes met.

Tears filled Ruth's eyes and she handed the note to Mary. She read it and hugged Ruth and they both cried. Ruth took the note back, folded it, and pressed it against her bosom.

The rabbis mounted the horses and Rubin carefully helped Ruth onto a horse. She held the bottom of her bloated belly and winced as she threw a leg over the back of the horse. Rubin was about to help Mary onto her horse but she deftly mounted on her own. Then he climbed on another horse and they all rode off.

The senators had settled into their usual chairs in the Curia Julia, the senate chambers. No one was talking and a sense of dread filled the air. Ever since Hadrian had slain a general in front of them, the senators had remained wary of the emperor whenever he appeared in the senate chambers. That was especially the case when the subject was related to the province of Judea. But today, Hadrian appeared buoyant and upbeat. After all, he was about to hear a great Roman victory. He was seated on a raised platform on his portable ivory curule seat and three Generals stood in front of him.

One of them stepped forward with a letter in hand. "It's from General Severus, your

Highness. Hadrian eagerly snatched it and opened it. With each passing second as he read it, his enthusiasm faded until the letter lay limp in his hand.

The general looked expectantly at the emperor. "General Severus was victorious, yes?"

Hadrian sadly nodded.

"Then I shall arrange a victory celebration."

Hadrian slowly shook his head. "The losses were too great. This is a day of mourning for Rome. I want to see a full report on the legions' losses as soon as possible."

The joyous sounds of a newborn baby crying filled the room. Ruth laid on a bed surrounded by midwives. One of them placed her baby, wrapped in a cloth, into her arms, and told her that it was boy. She was exhausted but elated.

"Let them come in," she said.

One of the midwives stepped out of the room and returned moments later with Rubin and Rabbi Akiva. They smiled warmly at her.

"Per Simon's wishes, I will name him Rufus."

"I wish Simon was here to see him," Rubin said.

Ruth smiles warmly. "He is."

Akiva was overwhelmed with joy. "Simon lives on in him. There is salvation for Israel yet."

Everyone smiled and Rubin pulled out one of the over-stamped coins from his pocket. He gazed at it as one would an object that brought good memories. He rubbed his thumb over it.

Epilogue

Jacob was tired from telling his astonishing tale. He gazed at the Bar Kochva coin, his prized possession that cost him a small fortune at the auction.

The mysterious man nodded with satisfaction. "That's quite a remarkable story." His gaze narrowed and looked at Jacob as if he were about to ask something personal. "Do you really believe it or do you think it's just a legend?"

Jacob smiled and stood up from the table where they'd been sitting in a small private room in the auction house. "I am a student and enthusiast of Jewish history. So yes, I do indeed believe it. At least parts of it. Besides, this coin is proof of it."

"Do you think the bloodline has continued?" the man asked as they walked out into the hall.

"Israel's history has never really known peace, so, it's hard to say if Simon's and Ruth's progeny has continued to the present."

"Well, if the story is true, it wouldn't surprise me." A couple of beats passed. "Thanks for the interesting tale."

The man shook Jacob's hand, then politely nodded and walked away.

"Excuse me," Jacob called after him.

He turned back."

"I never got your name."

"Oh, I'm sorry. It's Paul...Paul bar Kochva."

He smiled and winked at Jacob, then turned and walked away. Jacob stared after him, pleasantly surprised.

Postscript

Some scholars argue that the exceptional number of preserved Roman veteran diplomas from the late 150s and 160s CE indicates unprecedented conscription across the Roman Empire to replenish heavy losses within military legions and auxiliary units between 133 and 135. Those dates correspond with the Bar Kochva revolt. Legion XXII *Deiotariana* may have been disbanded after serious losses. It is plausible that Legion IX *Hispana* was among the legions that General Severus brought with him from Europe and that its demise occurred during Severus› campaign since it disappeared from history during the second century.

The size of the Roman army amassed against the rebels was much larger than that commanded by Emperor Titus sixty years earlier - nearly one-third of the Roman army took part in the campaign against Bar Kochva. It is estimated that forces from at least ten legions participated in Severus' campaign in Judea, including Legion X *Fretensis*, Legion VI *Ferrata*, Legion III *Gallica*, *Cyrenaica*, Legion II *Traiana Fortis*, Legion X *Gemina,* as well as cohorts of Legion V *Macedonica*, cohorts of Legion XI *Claudia*, cohorts of Legion XII *Fulminata* and cohorts of Legion IV *Flavia Felix*, along with 30–50 auxiliary units, for a total force of 60,000–120,000 Roman soldiers facing Bar Kochva's rebels.

www.ingramcontent.com/pod-product-compliance
Lightning Source LLC
Chambersburg PA
CBHW072122300726
48975CB00003B/884